WARNING
This book contains **HORROR** stories!

A Taste for the Macabre

Charles Black

Mortbury Press

Published by Mortbury Press

First Edition

2018

All stories original to this collection copyright © Charles Black

Cover art copyright © Steve Upham

ISBN 978-0-9556061-9-9

This book is a work of fiction. Names, characters, businesses, organisations, places and events are either the product of the author's imagination or are used fictitiously. Any resemblance to actual persons, living or dead, events or locales is entirely coincidental.

All rights reserved. No part of this publication may be reproduced, stored in a retrieval system, or transmitted, in any form, or by any means (electronic, mechanical, photocopying, recording or otherwise) without the prior permission of the author and publisher.

This book is sold subject to the condition that it shall not, by way of trade or otherwise, be lent, re-sold, hired out, or otherwise circulated without the publisher's prior consent in any form of binding or cover other than that in which it is published and without a similar condition including this condition being imposed on the subsequent purchaser.

Mortbury Press
Shiloh
Nant-Glas
Llandrindod Wells
Powys
LD1 6PD

mortburypress@yahoo.com
www.mortburypress.webs.com/

A TASTE FOR THE MACABRE

Lilly Finds a Place to Stay	7
The Accident	20
The Beast	30
Belt Up	42
The Con	55
The Collectors	69
Disciples of Evil	84
A Doggie for Christmas	92
Speak No Evil, See No Evil, Hear No Evil	103
First Love	115

'Lilly Finds a Place to Stay'
first published in
Kitchen Sink Gothic
(Parallel Universe Publications)
2015

'The Collectors'
first published as part of the
Vault of Evil Advent Calendar
2017

This book is dedicated to Charles Birkin.

LILLY FINDS A PLACE TO STAY

Lilly dressed quickly. She pulled on her clothes – panties, bra, tights, skirt, all black – aware she was under the scrutiny of Greg Haldane, who remained in bed smoking. She found the way he gazed at her unnerving, even though he'd just been intimate with every inch of her naked body. Her T-shirt was also black, apart from the white skull with blood-red blazing eyes on its front. Finally, she put on her trainers – Converse All Stars – and hurriedly tied the laces.

"Got somewhere important to go?"

"No."

"You seem to be in a hurry." Greg blew out a cloud of smoke. "Don't you like me?"

"Not really," Lilly muttered. Her answer could have applied to either of Greg's questions. The seventeen-year-old didn't particularly like him. Nor did she have anywhere specific to go, apart from anywhere that wasn't the squat. She was anxious to get away before any of the others returned. Other lads, that was.

"What was that?" Greg said sharply.

"Nothing."

"Sure." Greg's lip curled in a sneer. He didn't care whether Lilly liked him or not. He could have her whenever he wanted.

Any girls who lived in the house on Bird Hill Road were expected to have sex with any and all of the squat's male occupants. Not that they were

Lilly Finds a Place to Stay

told of this condition when they first moved in. However, it was soon made clear to them. That was bad enough. Worse was to follow, when, they were made to work the streets.

This wasn't what Lilly had expected when she'd run away with her boyfriend. Her relationship with her parents had been going downhill for some time. The first bone of contention was that they didn't like the music she listened to, or the volume that she played it at. Then it was her taste in clothes, the makeup she wore and the colours that she'd had her hair dyed: in turn black, purple, and then red. Her announcement that in future everyone had to call her Lilith hadn't been well received either. Finally, they didn't like the friends she'd started hanging around with. Especially Jase, who was five years older than she was. Far too old for a sixteen-year-old girl in the opinion of her parents. The arguments had grown more and more frequent, and Lilly hadn't needed much persuading when Jase had said she should come to London with him.

Everything had been great at first. Until Jase had met someone else, dumped her and kicked her out of the flat that they shared.

She moved in with Beth, a friend she'd made on Twitter some time before she'd left home. But things continued to spiral downwards. She lost her bar job after refusing to give the landlord a blowjob, and her money had soon run out. Beth

Lilly Finds a Place to Stay

proved to be not much of a friend when Lilly could no longer contribute to the rent.

Lilly should have gone home then. But stubbornly she didn't.

She'd met Greg at a gig. He'd said she could come and live in the Bird Hill Road squat. And she had.

Greg had got her into drugs. Sure, she'd smoked a joint every now and then, but Greg had got her onto the harder stuff. He'd started hitting her harder then too.

Greg suddenly jumped out of bed and grabbed Lilly's arm, squeezing tightly. "Make sure you bring some money home with you."

Lilly nodded meekly, and he let her go.

A few minutes later, she left the squat, walked down Bird Hill Road and onto Tanner Street. She didn't want to go to 'work'. She was sick of selling herself to the kerb crawlers who frequented Duckett Lane at any hour of day or night. She thought back to the argument when her father had said, 'If she dressed like a slut, she'd be treated like a slut.' She couldn't believe he'd said that at the time. 'I'm a Goth,' she'd angrily yelled back at him.

And now she was working as a prostitute.

Away from the squat, Lilly paused to light a cigarette. Instead of turning left, she went right, towards the shops. Perhaps she could get away with some shoplifting or pickpocketing.

Lilly's luck wasn't in. No sooner had she

Lilly Finds a Place to Stay

entered the shopping mall than she had attracted the attention of a security guard. Even though he was trying not to be obvious about it, it was clear that he was following her. She hadn't done anything suspicious, so Lilly supposed he must fancy her. Yes, he was definitely eyeing her up, paying close attention to her legs. She bent over, pretending to tie her shoelace. Looking between her legs, she could see he was enjoying the view of her bum in the tight black skirt. What a pervert!

If Greg had been with her, she could have acted as a decoy, distracting the guard, while he stole something.

She wandered around a bit more, went into HMV. There was a new CD she wanted, but the guard was still tailing her.

Frustrated, Lilly flounced out of the store and out of the mall. She ignored the shops on Tanner Street, and moved onto Sherton Street. It was starting to rain and rather than entering one of the shops she went into the library.

"Can I help you, dear?" The woman who sat behind the desk spoke with an Irish accent. The badge she wore indicated that her name was Mrs Margaret O'Riorden.

"Um, can I use a computer?"

"Are you a member?"

Lilly hadn't been in the library before, never mind filled in a membership card. She shook her head. "No."

Lilly Finds a Place to Stay

"I see." Mrs O'Riorden consulted her computer screen. "Sorry, dear. They're all booked up."

"Oh." Lilly stood for a moment thinking. "Got any books on serial killers?" She wasn't much of a reader, but this was a subject that interested her.

This caused the librarian to raise an eyebrow. "Serial killers?"

"Yeah."

The librarian smiled, and got up. "We have. I'll show you."

Lilly followed her deeper into the library.

"Here we are." The librarian indicated a shelf.

"Thanks."

Mrs O'Riorden smiled again and returned to her desk.

Lilly scanned the shelf. There weren't many, but there were enough to pass the time. Most were about Jack the Ripper, but there were also books covering Peter Sutcliffe: the Yorkshire Ripper, John Christie, Fred and Rosemary West, and Dennis Nilsen.

She pulled the books from the shelf and found a table in a quiet corner. The teenager quickly grew engrossed reading about some of the country's most notorious murderers and the victims of their grisly crimes. Most of whom were young women.

"Excuse me."

The librarian's voice made Lilly jump.

Lilly Finds a Place to Stay

"What?"

"We're closing up in ten minutes, dear."

"Oh. But it's just for the lunch hour, right? You open again at two though, don't you?"

Mrs O'Riorden shook her head. "No, sorry. It's half-day closing today."

"Oh. Right."

"Do you want to borrow any of those?" Mrs O'Riorden nodded at the pile of books on the table.

"Oh, um. No. Probably not a good idea."

The librarian frowned, then moved on to the computer room.

Lilly wondered if she dared hide somewhere in the library. She was in no rush to go back to the squat. But she was hungry, so she got up, returned the books to their shelf, and left the building.

It was still raining and she waited in the porch considering her options. She lit a cigarette and thought. She could get something to eat, but that would leave her with very little money and if she went back to the squat without any cash, Greg would hit her. She would have to go down Duckett Lane and pick up a punter. She wouldn't have any trouble getting one; there were always plenty of dirty old men who liked their girls young.

Lilly was still in the porch when the librarian emerged from the library.

Lilly Finds a Place to Stay

"Oh, hello, dear." Mrs O'Riorden locked the door and put the keys in her handbag.

Lilly caught a glimpse of a purse.

The Irishwoman tutted. "What dreadful weather." She looked Lilly up and down. "No coat?"

"No." Lilly shrugged. "I left it at the squat."

Mrs O'Riorden peered at the cloud-filled sky. "Doesn't look like easing off. You're going to get soaked."

Lilly sighed. "Yeah."

"Tell you what, dear, why not come back to mine? It's not far. And my brolly is big enough to shelter the both of us from the worst of the rain. I can lend you a coat."

"Um." Lilly frowned. The offer was unexpected, and she hesitated before answering, scrutinising the librarian. The woman had long brown hair, she wore 'sensible' shoes, and the clothes that Lilly knew she wore beneath her coat weren't what she would call fashionable, even for a woman of the librarian's age. And as for her age, she must be at least ten years older than her parents who were in their early forties. In Lilly's book that made her ancient. Ancient and not really a threat.

Mrs O'Riorden was speaking again. "My son's also interested in serial killers. He's got quite the collection of books about them. Certainly a lot better than the library's. You could take a look at them if you like."

Lilly Finds a Place to Stay

"Well." Lilly came to a decision. "Okay." She was suspicious of the woman's motives, but going with her was better than the alternative. With a bit of luck she'd be able to pocket something valuable. The contents of the Irishwoman's purse perhaps. Or maybe there'd be some cash lying around the house somewhere.

"Good." Mrs O'Riorden smiled and put up her umbrella. "It's this way. Come on."

Mrs O'Riorden was right: it wasn't far to her house, and they walked quickly and soon arrived there.

"Round here." She went to the back door and unlocked it. "Go on in."

Lilly stepped inside. Mrs O'Riorden shook her umbrella and followed the teenager into the kitchen.

"Now then. Tea? Coffee?" Mrs O'Riorden asked, once she had taken off her coat and hung it up alongside her handbag.

"Tea. Please."

"Sit yourself down then and I'll make us a pot."

Lilly sat at the kitchen table. As Mrs O'Riorden filled the electric kettle, Lilly's gaze went round the room. The kitchen was small and to her surprise, somewhat untidy. The shelves and worktops like the table were cluttered with all sorts of things: containers of various sizes interspersed with ornaments and trinkets. None of which appeared to be valuable. Perhaps there

Lilly Finds a Place to Stay

would be some money in one of the many pots. Or maybe the other rooms would provide better pickings.

Mrs O'Riorden rummaged in a cupboard and found a tin of biscuits. Lilly gratefully accepted when the librarian told her to tuck in to them.

"Milk? Sugar?"

Lilly nodded to both, her mouth full of chocolate digestive.

"Mmm, these biscuits are delicious."

"Glad you like them, dear." Mrs O'Riorden smiled proudly. "I baked them myself. My own recipe. Made with my special secret ingredient."

The tea was good too, made just the way Lilly liked it.

"So, you're living in a squat?"

"Yeah." Lilly took another biscuit. "I intend to move out as soon as I can find somewhere better."

"How did you end up there? If you don't mind me asking."

Normally, Lilly would have minded, but for some reason, this time she didn't. "Long story. Ran away from home is the short version." She wasn't going to go into details though.

"And do your parents know where you are?"

Lilly shook her head. "We don't get on."

"Ah. I had my share of troubles with mine."

"What about your son?"

Lilly Finds a Place to Stay

"Oh, when Sean was living here we had plenty of rows. Never causes me any trouble now though."

"This tea is the best I've had in a long time."

"Well, have some more then." Mrs O'Riorden refilled Lilly's cup.

Lilly sipped her drink. "And your son's interested in serial killers?"

"Oh, yes." Mrs O'Riorden laughed. "I can't think why. But the subject fascinated him. And so many books about them."

"Why didn't he take his books with him when he left?"

Mrs O'Riorden frowned. "I didn't say he'd left, did I?"

"Oh, sorry." Lilly was puzzled. She must've misunderstood the woman's Irish accent. "He still lives here?"

Mrs O'Riorden nodded. "He's still here."

"Oh." Lilly bit into another biscuit. This might make robbery more tricky, she thought. "Is he in?"

"Yes."

"Oh."

"You'll meet him in a bit."

"Right. What about your husband?"

Mrs O'Riorden's expression twisted into a scowl. "He did leave. The bastard!"

"Oh. Sorry."

The woman sighed. "It was a long time ago. Unfortunately, these things happen." She

Lilly Finds a Place to Stay

composed her features, her lips forming a smile again. "Now, you've had enough tea?"

"Yes. Thanks."

Mrs O'Riorden got up. "Well, come on through to the sitting room then." She started to lead the way, but paused and retrieved her handbag.

Lilly smothered a curse. She'd hoped the Irishwoman had forgotten that it hung within easy reach.

Lilly rose and followed Mrs O'Riorden. The hallway was narrow and made narrower by the cardboard boxes that were stacked the length of one wall. She suddenly felt a bit dizzy and staggered, steadying herself against the boxes. She wondered what might be inside them. She had her suspicions that it would just be junk.

"Is it that squat on Bird Hill Road where you are living?"

"Yeah."

"Aw, I've heard some terrible stories about what goes on in that place. It's no place for a girl like you to be living."

"I'm going to move out." Lilly reiterated her earlier statement. "Just as soon as I find somewhere better to stay."

For the second time that day, Mrs O'Riorden made an unexpected offer. "You should move in here. I've plenty of space for a little one like you."

Lilly wasn't so sure of that. The sitting room

Lilly Finds a Place to Stay

like the hallway was cluttered, not only with more cardboard boxes, but also plastic bags, both carrier and black bin ones. It was as she had suspected – Mrs O'Riorden was a hoarder.

"I've given a home to plenty of waifs and strays like you before."

Lilly was sceptical, though she didn't say anything.

"Sit yourself down and I'll go and fetch Sean down. You'd like that wouldn't you?"

Lilly smiled and gave the barest of nods. She was still feeling dizzy; sitting down would be a good idea. However, she didn't really want to meet Sean.

There was only one free seat though, and Lilly sat in it. The other armchair and the settee were both buried under a pile of stuff.

"I shan't be a minute." Mrs O'Riorden left the room, taking her handbag with her.

As soon as she heard her host going up the stairs, Lilly got up. She felt strange, unsteady on her feet, but she knew that this was her chance. If she was going to find anything worth stealing, she had to find it now. She picked a box at random and opened it.

"Oh my God!" She gasped in astonishment at what she saw inside. It was a skull. A human skull that sat on top of a pile of bones. In an almost mesmerised state, she opened another box. Another skull stared back at her.

Lilly Finds a Place to Stay

There were dozens of boxes; did they all contain bones? Lilly didn't care; she wasn't going to look in any more. She knew that it was time to leave. The problem was that she was having trouble moving properly. Her legs felt funny and her head was spinning.

Lilly lurched towards the door, reaching for the handle. She pulled it open.

Mrs O'Riorden stood in her way. "Oh, thank you, dear."

Lilly retreated unsteadily. Her mouth tried unsuccessfully to form words,

"Here she is, Sean." Mrs O'Riorden was alone. She was carrying a cardboard box. She entered the room and put the box down.

Lilly had backed up against the armchair. She swayed and collapsed into it. The special ingredient that her host had put in the biscuits was rapidly taking full effect. Soon, she would be unable to move at all.

"Sean." Mrs O'Riorden smiled and stroked the box. "This is Lilly. She's going to be staying here with us."

THE ACCIDENT

Gerald Simmington could feel the phone silently and persistently vibrating in his pocket. "Would you excuse me a moment?" He smiled at his companion at the bar – a rather shapely blonde called Vanessa – as he took out his mobile. "A very important client," he lied. "Need to take this call," he said truthfully. "Could net me a tidy sum," he lied again.

Vanessa pouted. Gerald liked the way she did that. "Don't be long," she said.

He winked at the girl then quickly slipped out of the noisy wine bar to the noisy street. The right sort of noise to be in the background when he spoke to his wife.

"What is it, Sylvia?"

"Gerry, darling, where are you? I've been trying to get you for ages."

"Stuck in traffic. There's been some sort of accident." Lies came easily to Gerald Simmington. "Caused all sorts of problems, so I'm running late."

Sylvia sighed. "Oh no."

"What's wrong?"

"Nothing's wrong."

"Why are you ringing then?"

"You haven't forgotten, have you?"

"No, of course not. Forgotten what?"

"We're supposed to be going out tonight."

"Mmm," Gerald's attention was distracted by

The Accident

the bottom and legs of a brunette wearing a short skirt who happened to be passing.

"Darling?"

"Hmm? No, I hadn't forgotten." He had. It came back to him now though. Dinner at Umberto's. "You managed to arrange a babysitter then?"

"Yes. Kathy from the village."

"Ah, the Fox girl, yes, I know." Gerald's imagination conjured up an image of the buxom nineteen-year-old redhead. The little tease was aptly named in his opinion.

Sylvia was speaking again; Gerald banished the image of the teenage babysitter.

"What's that, love? Didn't catch you."

"We'll still be able to go? Won't we?"

"Oh, yes, of course. Eight thirty, wasn't it?"

"Yes, that's right."

"Well, there you are then. Once I'm out of the worst of it I'll be able to put my foot down. There's plenty of time. I'll see you soon." Gerald smiled as he ended the call. Plenty of time for another drink with the delectable Vanessa.

That drink had turned into two before Gerald reluctantly decided he really had to leave the simply charming company of the very attractive blonde. Before he did so he gave her his number. His other number. The one for the phone that Sylvia didn't know about.

It wasn't that he didn't love Sylvia – he did – it was just, well, now that she was heavily

The Accident

pregnant he didn't find her very attractive. He knew that a woman in the full bloom of her pregnancy was meant to be beautiful, and some men did indeed think this, but Gerald didn't. And his eye started to wander. Even more than normal. Gerald wished Sylvia weren't pregnant. Wished he hadn't got her up the duff a second time. He hadn't meant to. It had been an accident. And it was Sylvia's fault really. She was supposed to take care of the contraception. Gerald didn't particularly like children. He'd fathered Timothy. Proved his virility. Produced the required son and heir. But really, one brat was enough. Of course, Sylvia had been delighted to find out she was expecting again. In her opinion it would be good for Timmy to have a little brother or sister. Someone to play with.

Gerald tossed his jacket onto the passenger seat, and rolled up his sleeves before getting into his Alfa Romeo. Turning the key in the ignition, he sighed when he realised that it was later than he thought. To get to his house in the country, wish Timmy goodnight, get showered and changed, and then back into town for dinner at Umberto's meant he really would have to put his foot down. Not that he minded driving fast.

Once out of town and the worst of the traffic his way was clear and he rapidly accelerated. Gerald had the car stereo turned up loud and the countryside passed in a blur to a soundtrack by the band of the same name. He smoked and sang

The Accident

along with Damon Albarn as the miles sped by. Then he was off the busy main route, and onto the rural road that would take him home. Traffic was sparse now. Gerald adjusted his speed to account for its twists and turns. But he hadn't adjusted it enough. Still driving faster than was sensible, especially under the influence of several drinks, Gerald allowed the car to drift to the centre of the road.

Gerald's concentration was momentarily distracted when fumbling in his jacket pocket for a new packet of cigarettes. Then his phone started ringing – the one Sylvia called – and almost too late he realised a white Transit van was heading straight for his car.

"Shit!" Yanking the steering wheel Gerald managed to manoeuvre the Romeo out of the van's way. He'd avoided a collision with the other vehicle, but he was unable to prevent the car from going off the road and onto the grassy verge. Gerald desperately slammed on the brakes, but it wasn't enough to stop the car from ramming into a dry-stone wall. The rear of the car went up in the air, and then came crashing back down.

The Transit van slowed briefly, then quickly sped away.

"Bloody hell!" Raymond Pulver had exclaimed when he saw the crashed car. As a travelling sales rep he made a lot of journeys up and down the motorways and A-roads, and he'd

The Accident

seen the aftermath of plenty of traffic accidents in his time. He always slowed down for a look but he'd never been first on the scene and in a position to stop and assist. He brought his Subaru to a halt, leaving the engine running he got out and ran to the overturned Alfa Romeo.

The front of the car was severely damaged and Pulver could smell petrol. As he peered through the window, he could see there was only one person in the wreckage. Even though the airbag had inflated the man's face was covered in blood. Pulver knew he was going to have to act quickly. He struggled briefly with the driver's door but it wouldn't open. He grabbed a stone that had fallen from the wall and used it to smash the side window.

He reached inside and felt the man's neck. "Oh, thank God!" he whispered. Gerald Simmington was still alive – Pulver could feel a faint pulse.

Pulver got his mobile out and took a photo of the unconscious driver. He returned the phone to his jacket pocket then grasped hold of Gerald's head and slammed it forward. He did it again and again, repeatedly smashing his face against the steering wheel, yelling, "Wake up! Wake up, you bastard!" as he did so.

As suddenly as he started he stopped. Moving back towards his Subaru, he pulled a box of matches from another pocket, struck one and tossed it beneath the wrecked car.

The Accident

Spilled petrol ignited and the Alfa Romeo quickly went up in flames. The matches went back in his jacket pocket and the phone came out again. He used it to take a photo of the inferno. Satisfied with his handiwork Pulver didn't hang around any longer. He'd achieved a long held ambition and he got the hell out of there.

"Oh, where are you, Gerry?" Sylvia Simmington was in the kitchen, anxiously checking the time. She was all dressed up with somewhere to go, but her damned husband hadn't turned up to take her. "Daddy really is a swine sometimes," she said, feeling her swollen belly. She supposed she shouldn't be surprised really. She had been surprised that Gerald had even agreed to take her to the exclusive restaurant. He probably regretted doing so. She could tell he didn't find her attractive in her present condition, even if she was wearing the most fashionable maternity dresses he probably didn't want to be seen with her in such stylish surroundings.

She tried his number. Eventually the call went to voicemail. Sylvia left a message. "Gerry, where are you? Ring me." Then for good measure she sent a text saying the same thing.

She finished her third glass of wine, and looked at the clock again. It was time Timmy was in bed. Too bad if he was asleep when Gerry got home. She went into the lounge where Timmy was playing with his toy cars and trucks.

The Accident

"Tim! Time for bed."

"Oh, mummy. Do I have to?"

"Yes!"

"But daddy's not home."

"He will be soon," Sylvia said with an optimism she didn't really feel. "He'd better be," she muttered to herself.

"What was that, mummy?"

"Nothing. Daddy's taking mummy out to Umberto's. So Kathy Fox from the village is coming to look after you."

Timmy's expression changed to a scowl. He didn't like Kathy. "I know. You told me earlier. I haven't forgotten."

"Unlike, it would seem, daddy."

"What?"

Sylvia sighed. "Nothing. Put your toys away now and get ready for bed. There's a good boy. I'll be up to check on you soon."

"Oh, all right then."

Timmy began to gather up his toys, and Sylvia returned to the kitchen and another glass of wine. She tried ringing Gerald again but got a number unobtainable message.

After ten minutes she decided it was time to tuck Timmy in. She tutted when she found him playing on the landing. "Tim! You're supposed to be in bed." He hadn't even changed into his pyjamas. Really, he was just like his father, never doing what he was supposed to. She hoped that the new baby would be a girl. She really

The Accident

ought to get a scan done to see what its sex was. For some reason, Gerald had said they'd rather not know. Sylvia suspected this was probably so he could pretend she wasn't really pregnant. An ignorance is bliss sort of thing, or something along those lines. Well, bugger him; she did want to know. She'd arrange to have an ultrasound; she didn't have to tell him the result, or even that she was having it done for that matter. She was sure he didn't tell her everything.

"Have you cleaned your teeth?"

Timmy flashed her a beaming smile. "Sure have."

"Well, that's something at least." Sylvia took her son's hand and led him into his bedroom.

"Mummy, I'm seven now. I don't need a babysitter." Sylvia let go of his hand and he went to sit on his bed, a serious expression on his face. "I don't need anyone to look after me. Especially Kathy Fox."

"Oh, is that so?"

"Yes."

"All grown up, are we?"

Timmy nodded. "I'm a big boy now."

"Right then, young man; show me just how grown-up you are. I'm going to the bathroom, and when I come out I expect you to be in your pyjamas."

"Yes, mummy."

She tousled his hair. "You're a good boy,

The Accident

Timmy." She smiled and left him to get changed. Sylvia realised she'd drunk more than she should have and going to the toilet was a pressing need.

Gerald still wasn't home when she finished in the bathroom, but at least Timmy was in bed. She kissed him goodnight then gathered up his discarded clothes, which were strewn all over the floor. She'd put them in the washer. There were some things in the master bedroom that could also be washed with them and she went to collect them.

As she was doing so the doorbell rang noisily and persistently. Perhaps Gerry had forgotten his key. She wouldn't put it past him. Sylvia hurried to see. Unfortunately, due to her baby bump and the bundle of washing that she carried, she didn't see the toy car that had been left at the top of the stairs. Sylvia trod on it. It caused her to stumble and with a shriek she went crashing down the staircase.

Outside, Kathy Fox had heard Sylvia's cry. She rang the bell and hammered on the door frantically. Getting no answer, she peered through the letterbox to see Sylvia Simmington lying at the bottom of the stairs with her head twisted at an unnatural angle. Kathy gave a gasp, took out her phone and dialled 999.

Timmy came running from his bedroom and down the stairs. He shook his mummy, but she didn't respond. "Wake up! Wake up, mummy!"

The Accident

he yelled. Tears were running down his face. It wasn't supposed to happen this way.

He rocked backwards and forwards next to his mummy, completely oblivious to Kathy's attempts to get him to open the door.

Timmy had been told that he should always put his toys away. Told he could cause an accident if he didn't. Daddy had said, "Imagine if he'd left something lying around and mummy had tripped over it, fallen and lost the baby. He wouldn't want that, would he?"

Actually, yes, he would. He didn't want to hurt his mummy. He loved his mummy. But Timmy didn't want a little brother or sister. Didn't want someone to play with. Didn't want to share his toys, or his mummy and daddy's love. Wanted to keep his parent's affection all for himself. That was why he had accidentally on purpose left his toy car at the top of the stairs.

THE BEAST

Helen Rutherford had just set off for a stroll with Rex her Border collie, when her mobile phone had rung. Its ringtone had sounded so out of place, as she walked down the lane that led from her new cottage to the village, and embarrassed by the burst of pop music, she had quickly answered the call to silence its discordant blare.

However, Helen was pleased to hear the voice of her best friend, Sandra Stanton.

"So how's it going then, this new life in the country?"

"It's wonderful, San'. So much green rather than the grey drabness of the city," Helen enthused. "So much open space rather than the looming, oppressive buildings. The trees, the birds, it's beautiful. The air is so clean; I'm feeling so much healthier. The people are so friendly; and you don't feel like you could be mugged at any moment."

"It sounds very nice, Hel', but I couldn't do without the cinema, nightclubs, restaurants, the pubs—"

"Hey," interrupted Helen, "we've got a pub. The Blue Boar, and very nice it is too!"

"Yeah, yeah. And what about the big shops? No department stores or fashionable boutiques. Are you sure you'll manage?"

"Oh, I'll manage. Besides high-heels and fancy frocks aren't really suitable for walks across the fields. You probably wouldn't approve of the fact that I'm wearing a pair of old trainers with a dress today."

"You're probably right!"

Helen laughed. "But seriously, San', I've definitely made the right decision. Moving to the country is the best thing I've ever done."

"Well, as long as you are happy."

"Oh, I am. And I can always come and visit you and the bright lights of the big city."

"You're welcome any time, you know that."

"And speaking of visits, you'll have to come and stay with me soon."

"I'd like that."

"We'll fix something up."

"Mark's been asking after you. He wants—"

"You won't tell him where I've gone will you, San'?"

"No, of course not." Sandra couldn't even pronounce the name of the remote Welsh village that Helen had moved to.

"Or anything else for that matter? Only he can be a persistent beggar."

"I promise I won't tell him anything. You should have confided in me sooner about the way he'd been treating you."

"I know. I know. But let's not talk about him. Tell me all the gossip."

"There's lots to catch up on," Sandra began.

She was in full flow with all the latest news about their mutual friends, when the call ended

The Beast

abruptly.

"Oh!" Helen examined her phone, waved it around a bit, but was unable to get a signal again. "Oh well, perhaps not everything is perfect," she said to Rex. She shrugged. "Never mind. Come on, boy." Not that Rex needed any encouragement.

She'd soon reached the village, and crossing the green, she decided to call in at the local shop.

She tied Rex up outside. "Won't be long," she told him, and went in.

Mrs Davies greeted her with a smile. "Morning, Helen."

"Morning, Mrs D. Lovely day, isn't it?"

"Yes, glorious."

"Just out for a walk with Rex. Thought I might take him up Caradoc Hill." Helen browsed the shelves, looking for something suitable for a snack.

"Up near John Merredith's farm?"

"Yes. There's some common land there, isn't there."

"Yes. Yes, there is."

"Then that's where we'll go." Helen made her choice of an apple, a nutritious cereal bar and a healthy energy drink. Once, she would have chosen a bar of chocolate, crisps and cola.

"Would you like a bag?"

"Yes, please."

Mrs Davies rang the items up on the cash register. "That'll be two pounds seventy-nine,

The Beast

please," she said, putting the items in a carrier bag.

Helen handed over the coins, wished Mrs Davies a good day and turned to leave.

"Helen, before you go," the shopkeeper called, "a word of advice."

"Yes?"

"Don't let Rex off the lead up there. John Merredith has had some sheep killed recently."

"Oh, how awful."

"Terribly savaged they were. And, well, like as not he's liable to shoot any dog that he sees loose."

"God!" Helen frowned.

Mrs Davies smiled reassuringly. "Like I say, as long as Rex is kept on his lead, you'll have no trouble."

Outside again, Helen untied Rex and headed towards Caradoc Hill. Her route taking her past the Blue Boar.

John Merredith was leaning in the doorway of the pub, pint in one hand, cigarette in the other, and a scowl on his face.

Helen smiled as she passed. "Morning, Mr Merredith."

The farmer's expression did not change. "You make sure you keep that beast under control, Missus," he called out.

Helen nodded, kept smiling and kept walking.

"Come on, Rex."

33

The Beast

Up the hill they went. Helen glanced back and saw that Merredith had stepped out into the middle of the road and was watching their progress. He spat on the ground. Helen hurried on. "Well, nearly everyone is friendly," she said to Rex.

Ahead, a sign indicated a footpath. Helen chose to take it, passing through the kissing gate, heading off the lane and across country.

There were no sheep about, but she kept Rex under control, even though it was clear he would like to be allowed to run free.

As she walked across the common land, Helen revelled in the glory of nature. There were so many different species of trees, flowers and birds to see. She had no idea what many of them were called. She would have to buy a book or books and gen up on such things, she decided.

Eventually Helen decided it was time to sit in the sun for a while and eat her snack. There was a stream just up ahead; perhaps she would dip her toes in its cool water.

When she found a suitable spot to rest, she settled down on the bank of the stream. "Sit, there's a good boy," she told Rex and began to take her trainers off.

As Helen's attention was distracted and she had momentarily let go of his lead, Rex seized his opportunity. And he was off, jumping over the stream, lead trailing behind him.

The Beast

"Rex! Come here, you naughty boy!" Helen shouted after him. But she wasn't really angry with him. After all, moving to the country was meant to give him a better life too. There were no sheep about anyway, so if he couldn't run around here, where could he?

And run around he did. Haring around like a mad thing.

Helen laughed at his antics. But then he suddenly changed course. He had picked up a scent and was following it.

"Rex! Come back!" Helen yelled after him. But he was away, all his attention focused on the scent.

"Damn!" Helen quickly pulled on her trainers and jumped over the stream.

Rex was out of sight now. He'd gone towards a small copse of bushes and willow trees. Helen went after him. The ground was softer here, wet, squelching under foot.

"Rex," she called again. "Where are you?"

There was no sign of the dog, and Helen pressed on, anxious now. She kept calling out to him.

He barked. Once, but no more. Still shouting for Rex to come back, Helen headed in the direction the bark had come from.

Helen was beginning to grow frustrated when she heard a crack or crunch. It had come from a tangle of bushes and brambles surrounded by lots of stinging nettles.

The Beast

"Rex, is that you?" Helen listened carefully. She thought she could hear something from the tangle. Yes, she was certain she could hear eating. "Rex, come out here now, you naughty boy." He must have found some old bones or a carcass. A dead rabbit perhaps.

"Rex, come here. Come here right now!"

She tried both a coaxing and a commanding tone, but the dog still failed to obey his mistress. Helen sighed. There was nothing else for it: she would have to go in and drag him out.

She pressed into the nettles, wincing as her bare legs were stung. "Rex! You are so in mummy's bad books," she muttered.

She reached the tangle of bushes. And tried to peer through them. Helen still couldn't see Rex, but she could definitely hear him, crunching, chomping on something. She thought that if she could at least spot his lead she could pull him out.

But there was no sign of it. Helen sighed again. "Oh, Rex!" It was typical that he would be somewhere deep in the briar patch.

There was nothing else for it, and she forced her way into the briars and brambles, thorns scratched her as she did so. At least she knew where to come when it was time to pick blackberries.

She suddenly paused, disgusted at the smell that reached her.

The Beast

"Uggh!" Her face wrinkled in disgust. "What have you got in there, Rex?" She worried that he'd found a dead sheep.

Then she spotted Rex's lead and she grabbed it. "Got you!" she exclaimed. "Out you come, my boy!"

She pulled on the lead, and was rewarded with an angry growl. "Rex! You come out now, you hear me?" She pulled again and was shocked to find herself yanked in return. "Ow! Rex!" Yanked so hard she was nearly pulled off her feet.

The growling was continuous now. "Whatever's got into you?" Normally Rex was such a good-natured animal. Helen decided there was nothing else for it, and pushed all the way into the heart of the bushes.

And stood stock still when she saw Rex.

Screamed when she saw what was eating Rex.

It was a man. A man who had pulled off one of Rex's hind legs and was chomping on it. Blood and drool dribbling down his chin and onto his blue-and-white checked shirt. His hair was long and straggly and the trousers he wore were brown corduroys.

He grinned at Helen.

Helen screamed again.

And the man pounced, grabbing her before she could even react. Such was her state of shock.

*

The Beast

"There you are, son," the white-haired old lady greeted her eldest, as he entered the farmhouse kitchen. "I been expecting you long since."

Her son took off his jacket and hung it up. "Aye. Been busy," he eventually replied in the surly tone that he habitually used.

The old lady nodded. "You'll want your tea?"

"Course." He sat himself at the kitchen table.

The old lady busied herself, filling a plate with food from the stove. She placed the plate before her son.

He began to eat ravenously. He always had a big appetite. "A brew wouldn't go amiss."

"Of course." His mother already had the teapot ready. "Could have done with your help today," she said as she poured.

"Oh?"

"I had to let Frankie out."

"You done what?" He thrust his fork aggressively into a sausage.

"I had to let Frankie out," she said again.

"Aye, I thought that's what you said."

"It's not right to keep him in all the time."

"No, I s'pose not."

"He was restless. Right agitated. So I had to let him out." The old lady seemed uncomfortable. As if she were having to convince herself that letting Frankie out was the right thing to do. "And he needs his exercise."

"Where is he now?"

The Beast

"I've locked him back in."

"He's not been getting up to mischief again, has he?"

"Well, that's what I could have done with your help with."

"Why? What's he done now?" The man sighed. "He's not been after the sheep again, has he?"

"No," the old lady hesitated. "He brought a lass home with him."

"He's done *what*?" her son roared, slamming his mug down on the kitchen table. Tea slopped out of it.

His mother wiped the table with a cloth, resisting the urge to tut. Her son had such a temper. It ran in the family. She smiled briefly as she remembered his father. "A lass—"

"Who was she?" he interrupted.

"Don't know. A stranger. Not from round these parts. Leastways, I hadn't seen her before. Pretty thing."

"Dead, was she?"

The old lady smiled. "Oh no. I think he's getting better."

His mind whirled, trying to decide if it really was better that Frankie had brought a girl home alive rather than dead. He rose, his meal unfinished. "I better see. Keep this warm for me."

The Beast

The old lady put his half-eaten meal in the bottom of the Rayburn, and followed him out of the kitchen.

They crossed the yard to the barn where Frankie was kept.

The old lady struggled with the lock. "It's me hands. The arthritis is bad tonight."

Her son snatched the key from her and undid the lock. He stepped inside.

The girl was still alive. Just.

"Aw," the old lady stood beside her eldest son, watching with an indulgent smile. "See, I told you he was getting better."

The son's mind was made up. It would definitely have been better for the girl if Frankie had bought her back dead.

Unlike his mother, he watched in distaste.

"It's good for your brother to have a friend," she said.

Now Frankie was dragging the naked, battered and bruised, almost-comatose Helen Rutherford around the barn using a dog lead that was attached to the collar around her neck.

"Frankie!" he shouted at his brother. "What have you done?"

Frankie paused. "'Er dog was loose on the common. Could've gone after the sheep. So I caught it." Frankie grinned. "Tasted right good, too."

"Frankie, I didn't have the sheep on the common today."

The Beast

But Frankie wasn't paying attention to what his brother was saying. "But she tried to take it from me," he went on. "So I caught her too."

John Merredith shook his head. "I told her to keep her bloody dog under control!"

BELT UP

As it was World Book Day, Jane had decided that they should all go into work dressed as a fictional character from a book.

Normally, Derek Barrowman would have been less than enthusiastic about having to wear fancy dress. However, not surprisingly for someone who worked in a bookshop, he did like books and reading, and for once, the prospect held some appeal. He spent a lot of time pondering which character he should dress as. He dismissed iconic figures such as Dracula or Frankenstein's monster, and, in the end, he settled on one that appeared in a short story by one of his favourite authors.

There was a box of old clothes in the attic that had belonged to his father when he'd been a young man in the 1960s. Remarkably, they remained free of the depredations of lepidopterans. And after rummaging amongst them Derek managed to find a pair of flared brown corduroy trousers and a vintage white shirt that would do for the character he had in mind.

But it was the belt that was the most important item of his costume. He wanted it to be as accurate as possible. After much searching, he customised two to make one. The first had probably belonged to a punk or a goth, he'd found it on a stall selling bric-a-brac in the

Belt Up

market. It was of black leather and had a large metal buckle with a grinning skull at its centre. The buckle was as close as he was likely to get, but the belt itself was wrong. His search for one that was suitable ended in a charity shop just off the Cheveley Road. This one was made of dark brown leather, and decorated with brass studs. Its buckle was plain and he replaced it with the one from the first belt.

To complete the look Derek didn't bother shaving that morning, and with the studs and buckle of his leather belt all polished and shiny he duly arrived at the bookshop. As usual, Derek was the first member of staff to turn up for work. Conscientiously, he got on with preparing things for what would be a busy day.

Angela Simpson arrived about five minutes before opening time. This was later than she was supposed to, but she knew she could get away with it as Jane had an appointment with her doctor and wouldn't be in until after ten.

"Well?" Angela did a twirl. "What do you think?" She was dressed as Snow White. And she had hired her costume from a fancy dress shop.

"Very impressive, Angela."

Angela smiled, pleased with Derek's reaction.

"Blimey! Who have you come as?" She looked him up and down, trying to figure out just who he might be. "Let me guess. Heathcliff, isn't it?"

"Er, no."

"Oh. I've got it!" Angela clicked her fingers. "Mr Darcy?"

"No. I've …"

"Don't tell me. You're someone from one of Charles Dickens's books. Must be."

"Wrong again, I'm afraid, Angela."

"Well, who then?"

"Barry Lane."

"Oh. Of course." Angela thought for a moment. "Who's Barry Lane? Character out of one those horror novels you like to read, is he?"

"Well, yes, although a short story rather than a novel."

He was about to tell her more but Angela had a customer to attend to. "Hang on, Derek."

"Excuse me." It was a teenage girl. "Do you have any new paranormal romances in?"

"Oh, just a minute." Angela had to check with her colleague. "Do we, Derek?"

"It's for my gran. She can't get enough of them," the girl explained.

"Yes. I put the new ones out this morning. Before you arrived, Angela," Derek said, pointedly. "I'll show you." He smiled at the girl and took her to the stand where the latest titles were displayed. "Here you are."

"Now, what were you saying, Derek?" Angela asked after the girl had made her purchases.

Belt Up

"Barry Lane, otherwise known as the Beast of Burslem, was the principal character in the short story of that title."

"Oh." Angela paused a moment, then said, "It's still horror though, isn't it? Something of an obsession with you, isn't it? Horror, I mean. I don't know how you can read that stuff. Sick, I call it. I've seen some of those films."

Derek looked puzzled. "Films?"

"Yeah, horror films." Angela tutted. "Reading horror books, watching horror films ..." She shook her head. "Torture porn, isn't that what they call it? Must have something wrong in the head if you like that sort of thing."

"I can assure you, Angela, there's nothing wrong in my head."

"Might kill someone one day."

"Just because I like to read horror stories it doesn't mean I harbour any secret desires to torture and kill people."

Angela burst out laughing. "Oh, I'm sorry, Derek. I'm only teasing."

"Oh."

"Nice belt, by the way." She bustled away to attend to another customer, leaving Derek to ponder whether she really meant that, or if she was pulling his leg again.

The morning followed a similar pattern, with customers still not really having a clue when they enquired what character he was supposed to

Belt Up

be. And in some cases, people assumed that he hadn't bothered dressing up at all.

The shop manager, Jane Moorcroft, arrived just before half ten. She was wearing a black dress decorated with white stars and crescent moons. Although Derek didn't think she'd made much of an effort with her costume, she had in fact made the dress herself, and Angela had praised it for its fine needlework.

Even so, Derek had no idea what character she was meant to be. However, it seemed he was the only one who didn't recognise that her outfit was inspired by a character called Celeste, from the book of the same name written by Niall Lord, and that it had been made into a popular animated movie. When this was explained to Derek, he remembered that Lord was Jane's favourite author.

There was a steady stream of customers throughout the morning, but when Derek was due to take his lunch break, Jane asked to see him in her office.

Derek followed her into the office and closed the door behind him. She was frowning when he turned round to face her.

Jane, who was sitting behind her desk, was already in something of a bad mood after being put on a special diet by her doctor. "Derek! I'm very disappointed in you. You haven't made any effort to dress up for World Book Day." She paused to take a breath. "In fact, you seem to

Belt Up

have taken it as an opportunity to make even less of an effort with your appearance than you normally do. You look like a tramp!"

"Well, I can think of a number of fictional tramps I could have come as. Frank Sarsfield from Russell Kirk's 'There's a Long, Long Trail A-Winding', for instance, but I'm not a big fan of Kirk's work."

"Derek!" Jane was growing impatient.

"But in this case I've come dressed as the Beast of Burslem."

"You what?"

Derek began to explain for the umpteenth time that day. "Barry Lane. The Beast of Burslem from the short story of that title."

"Oh." Jane shrugged. "I'm still none the wiser. Couldn't you have picked a more famous character? Harry Potter? James Bond?" She laughed briefly at the idea of Derek as the spy. "Bilbo Baggins perhaps?"

Derek frowned. "You never specified that it had to be a well-known character. Anyway, Barry Lane deserves to be better known. The story is undoubtedly a horror fiction classic."

"Well, who is this Barry Lane then?"

"He was a murderer known as the Beast of Burslem."

"A *murderer*?"

"Yes, that's right." Honestly, thought Derek, at times it was like trying to explain something to a child. "He terrorised the Potteries – that's the area around Stoke-on-Trent."

"I'm well aware of where the Potteries are, Derek."

"He strangled his victims with his distinctive belt. Very similar to this one in fact." He indicated the belt he wore. "I went to a great deal of effort to make it."

"Derek!" Jane wasn't interested. "Do you really think coming to work dressed as a murderer is appropriate?"

The question fazed Derek. He couldn't think why it would be inappropriate. "You've just said I could have dressed as James Bond; apart from the fact that he is 'licensed to kill' what's the difference?" He didn't wait for Jane to answer. "All you said was to dress as a fictional character from a book. I have. Actually, the story appears in two books. It was originally published in nineteen sixty-nine in *To Quake in the Night*, that's an anthology …"

"Derek!"

But Derek was in full flow and carried on talking. "Then in *The Taint of Evil* – a collection of stories by Charles Birkitt."

"Who?"

"Charles Birkitt. The author. He's one of the greats when it comes to short horror fiction. A veritable master of the macabre. Surely you must have heard of him?"

Jane shook her head.

Belt Up

Derek sighed. How did someone with so little knowledge of literature come to run a bookshop?

"I'm surprised, Jane, that you are not familiar with Birkitt. After all, your favourite author is on record as saying Birkitt's 'An Eye for Vengeance' terrified him when he was a boy."

"Really?"

"Alas, Mr Lord has also described Birkitt, quite wrongly in my opinion, as 'a terrible writer'. But then, again in my opinion, Mr Lord is something of an arse." Derek vividly recalled a book convention he had attended that the author was a guest at. They had both been in a crowded lift when someone had blown off. He was convinced it had been Lord.

"Hey!" Jane's face was red. "Niall Lord is the greatest writer of all time. And if he says this Berkett bloke, that no one apart from you has heard of, is a terrible writer, then he must be!"

"'The greatest writer of all time?'" Derek laughed. "How preposterous! You really are ill-read, aren't you, Jane?"

"How dare you?"

"And it's *Birkitt*, not *Berkett!*" Derek snapped. He had finally reached the end of his tether and he allowed years of bottled-up frustration to escape. "It's true though isn't it, Jane? It amazes me that anyone could think you are suitable to run a bookshop. It should be me running this shop. Not you!"

Belt Up

Jane remained remarkably calm. "But the fact is, I'm running it and I won't tolerate being spoken to in such a manner."

Derek glared at her, fists clenched.

"And as such, Derek, you're fired. Get out. Get out this instant!"

Derek leaned forward menacingly. "Bitch!" Then turned on his heel and left the office, slamming the door behind him.

Without a word to Angela, he walked out of the shop and into the rain.

The rain cooled his temper some. "What the hell have I done?" he muttered to himself as he walked down the High Street. The sudden aggressive outburst was out of character for the normally mild-mannered Derek.

On the other side of the road he could see the sign for the Golden Bell. Derek wasn't normally a drinker but, wet and miserable, he crossed over, stepped inside and without hesitation went straight to the bar.

"What'll it be, sir?"

"Brandy."

Jane Moorcroft's day had begun badly, but by the time she'd finished work her mood had improved. Sales were up, and although the incident with Derek had been unpleasant, his outburst was something of a godsend, giving her the perfect opportunity to get rid of him. With his passion for horror and true crime books he'd

Belt Up

always given her the creeps. All in all, it had turned out to be a good day.

Last to leave the shop, Jane had exited the premises by the rear entrance. She had just finished locking the door when she heard a noise in the alley that ran behind the building. She turned to see Derek staggering towards her. His expression was one of hatred.

"Derek! I'll scream if you come any closer."

At her warning, Derek stopped. He spat on the ground. "Bitch!" Such was the look of evil intent on his face that Jane hadn't noticed he had something in his hands.

It was the leather belt with the large buckle.

"Keep away or I'll call the police." She fumbled with the key, trying to get it back in the lock.

"Bitch!" The belt swung and the buckle struck the side of Jane's face.

She staggered at the blow and cried out in pain. Jane opened her mouth to emit a scream.

"Belt up, you bitch!" Derek rammed into her, slamming her face against the door, cutting the scream short. And then the belt was around her neck. Pulled tight and getting tighter. Jane gasped for breath, tried to scream, but her face was thrust against the door again even harder this time.

"Get inside." Derek had got the door unlocked and open and he bundled her through it. The door swung shut and he pulled the belt tighter

Belt Up

and tighter around her throat. And, as he did so, he was growing aroused. For the first time in months, Derek had an erection.

Derek was choking the life out of her, and despite Jane's struggles, which grew weaker and weaker, he didn't stop until some time after she was quite dead.

Eventually he let go of the belt and allowed her body to fall to the floor. He slumped beside her and pulled a bottle of brandy from his pocket. He drank long and deeply. The bottle was almost empty when Derek passed out.

Derek groaned when he regained consciousness. He rubbed his eyes, and Jane's body, the belt still around her neck, came into focus.

"Oh God! Oh God! What have I done?" But he knew what he'd done. It was all there; seared into his memory.

Derek began to cry. Why had he done it? He did not know. It wasn't like him. It was as if some devil had taken possession of him. But that was no excuse. The police would dismiss such claims. What should he do?

He reached over and removed the belt from around Jane's neck. Even so, when her body was discovered, he would be the obvious suspect. Lots of people had seen him wearing the distinctive belt and it would be obvious that Jane had been strangled with such an item.

Belt Up

Even if he were to destroy the evidence by setting fire to the bookshop, the finger of suspicion would still point at him. Angela would report that he had been sacked. Not that he had it in him to burn all those books. Yet he must act.

Derek knew what he had to do. He picked up the nearly empty bottle of brandy and walked to the stockroom. There was an old hook high up on one of the walls. Derek didn't know the reason for it being there. To his knowledge it always had been. It was a remnant left over from the time before the building was a bookshop. Whatever its original purpose was, it would do for his.

There was a kick stool nearby and Derek pushed it into position beneath the hook. He fastened the belt buckle so it made a noose, stepped up onto the stool and fixed the belt around the hook. He drained the bottle of its contents and let it fall to the floor.

Derek put his head through the noose and tightened it around his neck. He closed his eyes. He moved his right foot, placing it on the edge of the stool. Then he raised his left foot so he was on tiptoes and kicked the stool away with his right.

Slowly choking, Derek danced in the air, twitching, heels kicking against the wall. His tongue protruded from his mouth, and his face turned blue. For the second time that day, Derek got an erection. And as the supply of oxygen to his brain was cut off he slipped into unconsciousness, and eventually death took him.

THE CON

Jeff Frampton was driving home after finishing his shift at work. He had just joined the A361 near Pilton and ahead he could see a young woman standing at the side of the road.

It was beginning to rain and he slowed his red Triumph 1300 as he drew nearer. She was wearing a frilly white blouse and a blue full-length skirt.

Frampton brought his car to a halt beside her. He leaned over and wound down the passenger-side window.

"Need a lift?"

The girl smiled and nodded. "Uh huh." She was pretty and had an ox-eye daisy in her long blonde hair.

Frampton undid the door. "Better get in then."

The girl did so and made herself comfortable in the passenger seat. "Thanks."

"Where are you heading?" Frampton asked as he accelerated.

"Home."

Frampton grinned. "And where's that?"

"Glastonbury. Well, just the other side of Glastonbury is what I mean."

"Well, that's no problem."

"Great!"

"It's on my way."

"Where are you going?"

"Street."

The Con

"Oh, right. There's a lane just off the Street Road. You'll be going right past it. I live in the first cottage down it."

"It's your lucky day then. I can take you all the way."

"Cool! Thanks."

"What's your name?"

"Mary-Jane. And you are?"

"Jeff."

It was raining more heavily now. "Well, Jeff, you've saved me from a right soaking."

"Looks like it."

"Mind if I smoke?"

"No, go ahead."

Mary-Jane reached into her handbag and found a tin and a lighter. She opened the tin, took out a roll-up, put it between her lips and lit up. She placed the bag next to her feet when she'd put her things back in it. Frampton noticed that her shoes and the hem of her skirt were stained with mud.

"Is that a spliff?"

"Yeah. Want some?"

"Please."

Mary-Jane passed the joint over. Frampton took a drag and began to cough.

"You've not smoked one before, have you, Jeff?"

"Yeah, I have." Frampton sucked in some more smoke, and managed not to cough this time.

The Con

Mary-Jane giggled. "I don't believe you."

"All right, no I haven't." He handed it back.

"It's okay, you'll get the hang of it."

"So, you've been to the rock festival at the showground, have you?"

"That's right."

"How was it?"

"Amazing!"

"Who did you see?"

"Oh, lots. Fairport Convention, Pink Floyd, Donovan; he's so good-looking. Jefferson Airplane. And The Byrds, they were terrific."

"I'd have liked to have seen Led Zeppelin."

"Oh, they were really heavy, man."

"Yeah, I bet they were. What about the Moody Blues?"

"They didn't play."

"Oh, right."

"So, how come you weren't there?"

"I work at the hospital. Couldn't get the time off to go."

"Are you a doctor?"

Frampton thought about lying, girls always seemed to throw themselves at male doctors, but decided against it. "No."

"Well, it was really groovy, you should have skived off."

"Yeah, I suppose I should have."

Mary-Jane laughed. "You really are a square, Jeff. But I like you."

The Con

"Oh, right, thanks. So, you had a good time then?"

"Yeah."

"Lots of free love, was there?"

This time it was the girl who grinned. "Oh, yeah."

Frampton chanced a look at the girl. Her blouse was still damp and it clung to the curves of her body. He could see she wasn't wearing a bra.

Frampton licked his lips, imagining his mouth on her breasts. The car started to drift to the right.

"Oi, keep your eyes on the road!"

Frampton pulled the car back to the left.

"Don't suppose you've got any more of that free love to go round, have you?"

"For you, you mean?"

"Well, don't you think I deserve a reward for coming to your rescue?"

"Damsel in distress rewards her knight in shining armour. That what you got in mind?"

"Well, a knight in a shining Triumph, anyhow."

"Hmm, well, you are quite dishy for a square."

They were just entering Glastonbury; Frampton resisted the temptation to put his hand on her knee and switched on the radio instead. It was just past the hour and a news report was on air.

The Con

"*... Three people were killed in the crash,*" a male voice intoned. "*A convict has escaped from Her Majesty's Prison Cornhill, in Shepton Mallet. A police spokesman described Walter Trubnall as dangerous and under no circumstances should he be approached. Members of the public should contact the police if they see him. Industrial action. A further strike has been called—*"

"Same old doom and gloom. We don't want that on." Frampton reached to retune the radio to a station broadcasting pop music. He found one playing 'Suspicious Minds' by Elvis.

He suddenly laughed.

"What? What's so funny?"

"That escaped con."

"What about him?"

"Beyond being dangerous they gave no description. Do you think he'll be wearing a name-badge or carrying a big sign saying, I'm Walter Trubnall, dangerous escaped prisoner?"

"He'll be in prison uniform."

"Nah, he's bound to have ditched that. Pinched some clothes off someone's washing line."

"I suppose so."

Frampton grinned. "For all you know I could be him. Nicked some clothes and nicked this car."

"Stop it. That's not funny."

Frampton sighed. "No. It's not. I'm sorry."

The Con

"God! What a horrible thing to say." Mary-Jane shivered.

"It was stupid of me. I've always had something of a macabre sense of humour. Can we forget I said it?"

Mary-Jane shrugged.

"No wonder I ended up at the mental hospital."

"What?"

"Norah Fry's. It's where I work. I'm an orderly there, not a patient."

"Right." Mary-Jane sounded unconvinced.

"Really."

Frampton's flippancy had killed Mary-Jane's good mood. And, apart from the radio, they drove through Glastonbury in silence.

Mary-Jane broke that silence once they were out of the town and on the A39. "It's just up ahead. You can drop me off here."

"I'll take you to your front door."

"No, it's all right, this'll do."

"But it's still raining. It's no problem."

"There's not much room for turning round."

"I'm sure I'll manage."

"No," Mary-Jane said firmly.

"All right. If that's what you want."

"I do."

Frampton stopped the car at the entrance to the lane.

"But what about my reward?" He gripped her arm.

The Con

"Maybe some other time." Mary-Jane pulled free, opened the door and got out. "Thanks for the lift." She started walking quickly away.

"Damn!" Frampton cursed, he'd given the girl a ride, and had anticipated getting another sort of ride in return. Briefly, he contemplated following her. But he knew he'd be wasting his time.

It wasn't until he reached Street that he noticed she'd left her handbag in his car. He'd return it to her later and apologise. He'd give her a couple of hours to calm down first though. And just maybe he'd get what he wanted. After all, he reckoned he deserved it. He checked his watch. He just had enough time to pop to the florists and buy a bunch of flowers before they closed.

The short journey back towards Glastonbury didn't take long. He drove down the lane and soon came to a whitewashed cottage.

Frampton parked the car on the verge. He got out with the flowers and Mary-Jane's handbag, opened the gate, walked up the path through the garden, which needed some attention, and knocked on the front door.

There was no response, but he was sure he'd caught a glimpse of someone peeking out of an upstairs window as he'd approached.

He knocked again.

"Come on, Mary-Jane," he called out. "I'm sorry about before."

The Con

Eventually, just as he was about to try round the back, the door opened.

"Yes?" The man who opened it was tall and wiry; his hair was short and his face hard. He looked Frampton up and down, frowning when he saw the handbag and flowers.

Frampton spoke first. "Erm, hello."

The man didn't say anything, waited for Frampton to explain what he wanted.

"I was looking for Mary-Jane."

"Was? You mean you aren't any longer?"

Frampton frowned. "No. I'm still looking. Is she in?"

"I don't know anyone by that name."

"Mary-Jane, she lives here."

"No, she doesn't."

"She does. I gave her a lift earlier. Dropped her off at the end of the lane."

"Did you now?"

"Yes. She said she lived in the cottage, which I presume is this one, seeing as there are no other buildings here."

"There's only me living here now."

Frampton wondered if Mary-Jane had been so anxious to get away from him that she'd told him that the first lane they'd come to was the one she lived down.

The man was making to close the door and Frampton put his hand on it to stop him from doing so. He described Mary-Jane, "Pretty girl, slim, long blonde hair. Early twenties, I'd say."

The Con

"Oh, her."

"Yes?" Frampton waited expectantly.

"There used to be a girl like that who lived here. Not any more though."

"But she can't have moved out just like that, surely?"

"I didn't say she had, did I?"

"No," Frampton admitted. "But what—"

The man interrupted. "She's dead."

Frampton looked aghast. "Dead? But how? When? What happened?"

"You'd better come in." The man stepped aside to allow Frampton to enter. "Go on through." He pointed to a door that opened to the sitting room.

The man followed him in and allowed the door to swing shut. "You'd better sit down."

Frampton sat in one of the armchairs. The man remained standing. He leaned back against the door.

"You gave her a lift earlier, you say?"

"That's right. Wait a minute, you're not going to tell me a girl like that used to live here years ago and that I gave a lift to a ghost, are you? Because, well, for one thing, I don't believe in ghosts. And for another, she left her bag in my car." Frampton held the handbag up.

The man smiled. "I wondered why you were carrying that."

"I wanted to return it."

"I bet."

The Con

"I beg your pardon?"

"Pretty girl, you said."

"I did. Look, just what are you implying?"

"More to you turning up here than to just return a handbag, I reckon."

"I don't like your tone."

"I'm right though, aren't I?"

Frampton was growing exasperated and he wanted some answers. "What exactly is going on here? You said Mary-Jane was dead. How's that possible? She was fine when I dropped her off. And for that matter who are you anyway?"

"She was pretty. Mind you, any woman would look pretty, if you'd been locked up as long as me."

"What?"

"You heard what I said."

Frampton had started to rise. "You're Trubnall! The escaped convict."

"Of course I am." Trubnall smiled, his hand went behind his back and he pulled out the knife that he had in his belt. "Now sit back down." He pointed the knife at Frampton.

"What have you done to Mary-Jane? Where is she?"

"I raped her."

"You bastard!" Frampton swore.

Trubnall didn't seem offended by the insult. "What's the matter? That's why you came here, wasn't it? You wanted to screw her, didn't you?"

Frampton shook his head.

The Con

"I raped her. Raped her repeatedly. She put up quite a fight for a hippy. Thought they believe in peace and love. Mind you, that made it all the better."

"Oh my God!"

"Then I killed her."

"Oh God!"

"I didn't mean to. Just she struggled a bit too much." Trubnall laughed. "So, yeah, I killed her. And then I raped her again. See, another thing you learn when you've been locked up is to take your pleasures where and when you can."

Frampton felt sick. "You're a maniac!"

"I wasn't when I went inside. They made me like this. They turned me into a maniac." Despite admitting this, Trubnall seemed perfectly at ease, confident that the young man held no threat to him.

As the escaped prisoner spoke, Frampton was looking desperately around the room. There was only one door out and Trubnall had that blocked. Perhaps he could try diving headfirst through the window, but no, Trubnall would stop him before he could reach it.

Suddenly, Frampton blurted out, "Look, just let me go and I'll say nothing. I'll forget all about seeing you and coming here." It was obvious the criminal wouldn't just let him go, but it was a tack he had to try, otherwise he was going to have to fight the maniac. He would need a weapon; unarmed against a knife he stood no

The Con

chance. As far as he could see, a large brass candlestick was his best option.

"Let you go? Now, why would I do that?"

As Trubnall pondered this, Frampton made a grab for the candlestick.

"Hey!" Trubnall yelled.

Improvised weapon in hand, Frampton charged at the criminal. He swung the candlestick and Trubnall stuck the knife out in front of him. Frampton's momentum carried him onto the point of the knife, and the heavy ornament connected with Trubnall's head. Frampton cried out in pain; Trubnall fell to the floor, pulling the blade from between Frampton's ribs as he did so.

Frampton couldn't believe it, he was wounded, bleeding quite badly, but he had bested the criminal. Trubnall was unmoving, slumped against the door. Frampton grabbed a cushion and pressed it against his wound, and knelt to check Trubnall's condition. He'd assumed his opponent was unconscious, but he didn't seem to be breathing.

"Oh God, I've killed him!" One-handed, he pulled Trubnall out of the way. "It was self-defence," he muttered. "Had no choice. Had to do it."

Frampton groaned. He was really in some pain now. He must have been hurt worse than he'd first thought. He'd already noted that there was no telephone in the sitting room. He opened the

The Con

door, hoping to find one in the hallway, but there wasn't one there either.

Frampton staggered outside. To see a ghost.

"Hello, Jeff."

"Mary-Jane?" Frampton stared in open-mouthed astonishment.

"Who else?"

"But Trubnall said …"

Mary-Jane laughed. "He's good, isn't he?"

"Who? What? I don't understand."

"My friend Ray. He's an actor. Specialises in improvisation."

"But …"

"I'd told him all about you, and when we saw you arrive, well, Ray decided he would play a trick on you. How does it feel to be the victim of someone's macabre sense of humour?"

Frampton swayed.

"Are you okay?"

"Trick? I …"

Frampton abruptly collapsed.

"Oh my God, you're hurt! What happened in there?" Mary-Jane ran over to where he lay. "Ray! Ray, get out here!"

Of course, Ray couldn't hear her. However, someone else could.

The real Walter Trubnall had stolen a car belonging to a festivalgoer, but he hadn't gone far before it had broken down. Upon abandoning it, he had travelled on foot across country. He'd been intending to steal the red Triumph parked on the verge when he'd heard the woman's voice.

She was obviously in some distress.

Trubnall hadn't had a woman in a long time.

Soon she would be in even more distress.

THE COLLECTORS

Every time the lash of the whip bit her back, the young woman screamed in agony. Dennis Varley's grin bordered on maniacal. The classical music soared; it was proving the ideal accompaniment to the woman's screams. Oh, how he was enjoying this! Again and again the whip viciously tore at her back. Varley groaned in pleasure, then groaned in dismay as the tortured woman's cries were suddenly augmented by the ringing of a telephone. Of all the times to be interrupted!

The answer machine clicked into life.

"Varley? Varley, are you there?"

Dennis Varley groaned again. The woman was whimpering, tears running down her pain-contorted face, gasping in agony. Oblivious, the orchestra played on.

Varley had recognised the voice immediately. In fact, he could have correctly identified the caller before he'd even spoken and that was without the aid of caller ID. It was Anthony Pendle, widely acknowledged as *the* expert on horror anthologies. The widely acknowledged expert who frequently consulted Varley on that very same subject.

"Pick up, Varley." Pendle's voice had a wheedling tone.

This was the second time that Anthony Pendle had called Dennis Varley that day.

The Collectors

Pendle's earlier phone call had been to suggest that Varley should publish a book of horror stories that had a lavatorial and scatological theme. "It'll scare the shit out of you!" Pendle had suggested for a promotional tagline.

Varley had thought it was a viable project but hadn't admitted that to Pendle, telling him he would think about it. Varley had already come up with a title for it – *The Stench of Fear*.

Dennis Varley was a frustrated horror writer; every story he had ever submitted for publication had been rejected. Even the ones he had sent to *for the love* publications.

As a result of this he had founded his own publishing company, specialising in horror anthologies. And in every anthology he published, at least four of the stories were written by him, and each one credited to a different pseudonym.

Despite the fact that the critics largely dismissed Varley's anthologies as being of little literary merit, of containing violent pornography, and for appealing to the lowest common denominator, they actually sold quite well.

Pendle was persistent. "Pick up, Varley. It's important!"

Varley sighed, and reached for the landline. Perhaps Pendle was ringing to find out Varley's verdict on his anthology proposal. "Hello, Anthony."

The Collectors

"Hello? Varley? Varley? Good grief! Can't you turn that racket down?"

"*Racket?* That's no racket," bellowed Varley. "It's—"

Pendle butted in. "Whatever it is, I can hardly hear you over it!"

Varley sighed again. "Oh, hang on. I'll take the call in the library." Muttering, Varley put the phone down, left the room, closing the door behind him, and went to his library. He took his time – he wasn't paying for the phone call.

Once he had sat in his overstuffed club chair, and gazed lovingly at his crammed-full bookshelves, he picked up the receiver of the library extension. "What is it, Anthony?"

"I'm just ringing to pick your brains about something."

Varley grunted, thinking he'd like to pick Pendle's brains, quite literally.

Both men collected horror anthologies from the heyday of horror publishing, and anything connected with them – cover art, promotional material, even reviews. And whilst both men shared this interest, and both were also firm advocates of real books rather than their electronic equivalent, Varley harboured feelings of loathing for Pendle. Not that Pendle was alone in being loathed by Varley.

Varley didn't really like people. No, that was putting it mildly; rather, he despised the human race. And people (especially women) didn't

The Collectors

really like Varley. He was unpopular and unattractive. Whereas Anthony Pendle *was* popular and attractive. And never short of female company.

And at heart (black and twisted), Varley was a sadist. All of the stories he wrote reflected this.

"What is it, Anthony?"

"Do you remember I told you that on the back cover of *The Thirteenth Satyr Book of Horror Stories* the quote from Edmund Maitland's 'Cold to the Touch' was mistakenly credited to an Emma Astley?"

Varley grunted in annoyance. "Actually, it was I that pointed that out to you!"

Pendle ignored Varley's rejoinder. "Well, I popped in to a jumble sale at the local church hall today, and came out with an old hardback anthology of ghost stories. One I'd never heard of before."

Varley had a sinking feeling; he knew what Pendle was going to say next.

"It's called *From the Grave*."

Varley ground his teeth in annoyance. *From the Grave* was very, very rare, and he had long coveted a copy.

"It only cost me ten pence!"

"Congratulations," Varley managed to say, but in reality he was seething.

"Anyway, looking down the table of contents I spotted that there's a story called 'An Angel Dying' by Emma Astley."

The Collectors

That was the reason why Varley desired the book so much.

"Not only that, unlike *The Satyr Book of Horror Stories*, there are biographical notes about the authors."

Varley knew this too.

"What does it say about Astley?" he asked eagerly.

"Not much, certainly no mention of the *Satyr Books* or Edmund Maitland, or any other pseudonyms for that matter—"

"Well, that's not surprising," Varley interrupted, "as *From the Grave* came out before the first *Satyr Book of Horror Stories* was published!"

"Oh, of course."

"So what does it say?"

"Um, it's got a date of birth – nineteen thirty-seven – and says that she lives in Cornwall."

"That's it?"

"'Fraid so. At least there's a chance she's still alive."

"Yes, I suppose so. Have you read the story yet?"

Pendle laughed. "I have; it's right up your street! It's about torture and murder in St Ursula's convent that leads to a ghostly revenge. Would you like me to read it to you?"

"No!" Varley spluttered. Pendle liked to think he was something of a gifted orator. He was

The Collectors

alone in that opinion. Varley wasn't prepared to listen to him drone on and on. "Um, I'm afraid there's someone at the door," Varley lied.

"Okay. I'll make you a copy. Send it to you."

Varley wasn't going to hold his breath. Pendle often said he would send him something, only not to follow through.

But for once, Pendle had been as good as his word and made Varley a copy of 'An Angel Dying'. As he read the story, Varley's thoughts began to race. He had grown up in Cornwall. His school had been called St Ursula's, and it was on the site of what had once been a convent.

It was as a child that he had first started reading horror anthologies. His particular favourites had been the long running *Pan Book of Horror Stories*, and *The Satyr Book of Horror Stories*, a series that had all too evidently been created to cash in on the popularity of Herbert van Thal's anthologies.

His favourite author was the prolific Edmund Maitland, whose stories featured sadism, horrific cruelty and torture, and regularly appeared in *The Satyr Book of Horror Stories*.

At this young age, Varley had been inspired to write his own stories too. However, neither his choice in reading material nor his efforts at fiction had met with the approval of his English teacher.

The Collectors

His English teacher who all too readily would resort to corporal punishment when she caught him reading one of his lurid paperbacks or when he persisted in writing his own horrific tales.

His English teacher whose name was Mrs Astley.

Was it possible?

Varley didn't know her Christian name, he and his school friends had always called her 'Ghastly Astley', but the date of birth would be about right.

Was her name Emma?

No, it couldn't be.

Could it?

Was Ghastly Astley also Edmund Maitland?

He would find out. He had more of a lead than Pendle, who would still be checking telephone directories. Even if she were still alive, she wouldn't necessarily still be living in Cornwall. Would she?

He would pay a visit to the West Country and see what he could discover. But first, he had to deal with the young woman he had chained up in the other room. Fiona Hudson was an author who had contacted him about writing for his anthologies.

Dear editors, she had written.

I'm a new horror writer and a big fan of your series of horror anthologies. New horror writer she may be, but if she was such a big fan of

The Collectors

Varley's books, she would know that he, and he alone, edited them. *I was wondering if I could submit to you. If so, please send me submission guidelines.*

Varley had checked out her website – in particular her photo gallery – liked what he had seen, and replied to her enquiry, inviting her to meet him. Seizing on the networking opportunity, Hudson had accepted.

She had hoped such a meeting would lead to her getting a place on Dennis Varley's roster of contributors, not hoisted in chains in his torture chamber.

The classical music had finished by the time Varley had returned to his room of pain. He could hear his victim mewling. Varley sniffed in disdain, and noted that she had soiled herself. He tutted, changed the compact disc, and picked up his favourite meat cleaver. Varley smiled as the music began. It was time to make some editorial cuts.

The little Cornish town had grown larger since Varley had lived there in the 1970s, but, in the end, it hadn't proved hard for him to locate his old teacher, Mrs Astley, as she was still living locally.

Not surprisingly, she had retired from teaching, though Varley was surprised that she wasn't a resident in an old people's home, but

The Collectors

living in a cottage on the outskirts of Porthpetroc.

Varley decided to practise a deception when he visited his former teacher. "Mrs Astley? I'm Anthony Pendle."

"Oh, yes, you rang me. I hadn't expected to see you so soon, Mr Pendle. Do come in."

So Pendle *had* tracked her down too. Good job he hadn't hesitated in making the long trip to Cornwall then.

"Take a seat," she invited.

Varley settled himself in an armchair. "It's good of you to see me, Mrs Astley," he said – although, the way in which she peered at him indicated that her sight was failing. She seemed to have shrunk as she had grown older too. He hoped she wasn't senile; at least, not completely.

"Can I get you some tea, Mr Pendle?"

"That would be nice, milk, with two sugars, thank you."

"Excuse me a moment." Mrs Astley busied herself in the kitchen.

She returned with a cup of tea for each of them, and asked, "What was it that you wanted to see me about, Mr Pendle?"

"It was about your writing."

"My writing?" Mrs Astley frowned.

"Yes, you are Emma Astley, aren't you? The author of 'An Angel Dying'?"

"Oh," Mrs Astley gasped. "Yes, I am, although that was a long time ago now."

The Collectors

"Did you write anything else?"

"Anything else?"

"Yes, in particular I'm wondering about a story called 'Cold to the Touch'."

"Oh!" For a moment Mrs Astley seemed lost for words. Then she began to laugh, or rather cackle. "I was most annoyed when some idiot made that mistake on the back cover. Yet, you are the first person to ever put two and two together. Did you also notice I never wrote for that series again after that?"

"Yes, and the *Satyr Books* were never as good."

Mrs Astley cackled again.

"I took the liberty of bringing some books with me; would you mind signing them for me?"

"Very well, Mr Pendle, I've never been asked for my autograph before, and once I would have denied all knowledge of such matters, but I shall reward you for your diligent research."

She reached for a pen, and Varley began to unpack the books from his bag. Despite their age all were in near mint condition.

"Oh, you have two of each volume?"

"Yes, could you sign one copy for me and the other for my friend and fellow enthusiast Dennis Varley?"

"Very well." She began to inscribe the books, then suddenly paused. "Dennis Varley? That name seems vaguely familiar."

"Really?"

The Collectors

"Yes," Mrs Astley appeared about to say something more but evidently changed her mind, frowning instead. "I cannot think why."

"Oh, what a shame."

"Quite. But memory loss is one of the banes of old age."

Mrs Astley had finished signing the books now and was massaging her wrist. "Arthritis is another."

"Yes, I'm sure it must be quite painful." Varley had packed half of the books back in his bag. "As will this be," he said, taking out his meat cleaver.

"What? What are you doing?" Mrs Astley opened her mouth to cry out, but Varley's punch knocked the old lady over before she could emit her shriek.

She lay sprawled on the floor, her false teeth broken, shaking her head, whimpering in fear. Smiling, Varley knelt beside her and with a deft swipe of the meat cleaver, the editor made his cut, and Mrs Astley did scream then.

Varley had chopped off her right hand.

The hand that she had used to sign his books. Even if she didn't bleed to death, she'd never sign any more autographs, so the value of the books in his bag had just increased even more.

The hand that she had used to inflict corporal punishment on him when he was a little boy.

Of course, the stories he'd written as a child were not very good, but he'd often wondered at

The Collectors

the brilliance of Edmund Maitland, who had seemingly similar ideas to his, and also the skill to execute those ideas with far more panache than the young Varley could.

Varley decided that in order to point the finger of suspicion at Anthony Pendle he would leave the books signed to him behind. However, he would keep his old teacher's hand. His long journey home should give him enough time to decide which of his collections Mrs Astley's hand would best belong in.

Anthony Pendle knocked repeatedly at the door of Mrs Astley's cottage. No one came to answer it. He tutted impatiently. She must be getting on a bit. Probably couldn't move very quickly, he thought.

He pushed open the letterbox and called through it, "Hello? Mrs Astley? Is there anyone there?" Pendle tutted again. She'd probably forgotten to put her hearing aid on.

But he thought he could hear something. Only faintly mind. He banged his fist upon the door again. Still no one came in response.

He moved to the window and peered through it. He gasped when he saw what looked like someone lying on the floor. The old dear must have had a fall. Pendle quickly returned to the door, and forced it open.

"Jesus!" Pendle swore when he saw the blood. And he swore more vehemently when he saw the reason for the blood. Amazingly, she was still alive, but barely clinging on to life. Pendle grabbed an antimacassar and wrapped it around the end of Mrs Astley's arm, trying to staunch the flow of blood.

He was just about to press nine for the third time on his mobile phone when he spotted the pile of horror anthologies. Unable to resist, he flicked open the top copy and was surprised to find it was inscribed to him. As were the others. How wonderful! He hadn't told Mrs Astley why he wanted to see her, but she must have heard of him already and signed a set of her personal copies of *The Satyr Books of Horror* just for him. Well, he reasoned, why wouldn't she know who he was? After all, he *was* the renowned authority on horror anthologies.

But how, he wondered, did Mrs Astley come to be in this condition?

The old lady was trying to say something now and he leaned closer to hear.

"Pendle … An'ny Pendle …"

"Yes, Mrs Astley, I'm here. What happened? Who did this to you?"

"Pendle … An'ny Pendle … Attacked me … cleaver …"

The old bat was clearly delirious. And then Pendle had a sudden insight. He knew with certainty that Dennis Varley was responsible. Who else could it be? The crazy bastard! Varley

The Collectors

had finally flipped and was trying to outdo Pendle.

Pendle could just imagine Varley gloating, thinking he'd got one up on him. The sick bastard would probably be masturbating over his trophy. Hell, he could imagine Varley using his trophy to ... No! He tried to banish that unwholesome image from his mind.

Well, Varley might have taken the hand that wrote the Maitland stories as the ultimate collector's item, but however extreme an act that might be, taking just Mrs Astley's hand was typical of Varley. He lacked real vision. He never seized an opportunity with two hands and took full advantage of it.

Unlike Anthony Pendle.

It was an outrageous idea, but, yes, he would do it. Varley had taken the hand; Pendle would take the writer. He would add *Mrs Astley* to his collection of horror memorabilia!

It would be like that story. He couldn't think of the title. Was it by Bloch? Or perhaps Syd Bounds? Varley would know of course. Varley always knew.

It was a good job he hadn't made the call to the emergency services, he thought. She'd lost a lot of blood and would probably die before an ambulance arrived anyway. But Pendle knew what he had to do. It was better this way.

First, he had to stop the bleeding.

The Collectors

As he ran into the kitchen to prepare things, his mind was racing with the possibilities. He had a complete set of signed books. He'd be able to take a photo of himself with the author and add it to the gallery on his website. He could keep the author herself in his basement.

His operating theatre prepared, Pendle ran back into the front room with the cable from the electric kettle, which he used as an improvised tourniquet.

The old lady was groaning softly, and as he wasn't a sadist like Varley, he used a meat tenderiser to knock her out. Once she was unconscious, he picked her up and carried her into the kitchen.

Pendle had switched the electric cooker on and turned one of the hobs up so it was set to maximum heat.

The hob was red-hot now and Pendle took hold of the old lady's arm and pressed it against the hob, using it to cauterise the stump.

The smell was most unpleasant. And unfortunately, Mrs Astley had added to the stench by soiling herself.

"Flaming hell!" Pendle shouted.

As he had feared, it had all proved too much for the old lady and she had given up the ghost.

Pendle sighed. "Oh well." He wasn't to be defeated though. He could always try his hand at taxidermy.

DISCIPLES OF EVIL

When the soldiers from the Death's Head unit ordered Klein from the barrack hut that chill morning he expected to be performing his usual duties as one of the camp's *Sonderkommando*.

A transport train had recently arrived laden with prisoners, and, at the urging of the SS guards, the new arrivals were rapidly disembarking from the cattle wagons. The selection process was already underway. This cursory inspection decided who was fit to work and who would be executed. To the right, the able-bodied were marched away to slave in the labour camp; the others were told that they were going to the shower block to be disinfected.

To Klein's surprise, rather than accompanying those who were really destined for the gas chambers, the two guards marched him to Block 18. This was a part of the camp that he had not been in before, and despite eighteen being considered a lucky number by the Jews, there was no good fortune associated with this building. There were rumours that the Nazis conducted strange experiments on prisoners in this building; and although he was relieved that for once he wouldn't be involved in the deception that was being played upon those sent to the left, Klein did not relish finding out whether these rumours were true. They walked along a corridor until they reached a door where another soldier stood on duty. The sentry – *SS-Unterscharführer* Otto Hartmann – knocked on the door, and a voice commanded, "Enter."

The room Hartmann pushed Klein into was quite spacious, yet the other two guards remained outside the door.

Klein's gaze darted around the room. The man sat behind the desk he did not know, but he knew enough to know this was a man to be feared even more so than the rest of the Nazi pigs. Brunner was the name of the soldier watching the two women who stood huddled together in a corner. Klein knew both of them very well. He was surprised by their presence, yet no matter how much he wanted to, he knew better than to say anything when he saw them. He waited for the seated man to speak.

The Nazi wore a white laboratory coat over his black uniform, and was reading a file. He was *SS-Hauptsturmführer* Dr Franz Von Gruber. He did not look up when he said, "You have all worked hard in the labour camp and now you are to be rewarded for doing so."

SS-Hauptscharführer Brunner smirked at this.

Eventually Von Gruber looked at the prisoners, his gaze finally settling on the man. "You are Alfred Klein?"

Klein hesitated momentarily before nodding his shaven head.

"And these are your wife and daughter." The Nazi indicated the room's two female occupants.

Disciples of Evil

He was a handsome man, but his good looks were temporarily marred by an expression of evident distaste.

Alfred Klein had not seen his family in some time as they had been immediately separated upon their arrival at the camp, and although the abuse and degradation they had suffered during their internment had changed them physically, he had recognised them both instantly. The Jew made to shuffle towards them, but Hartmann thrust his rifle out blocking his path.

Dr Von Gruber checked his notes. "Miriam and ..."

"Lisabeth," Klein whispered. The girl who had been his beautiful teenage daughter had aged years. It was as if a lifetime had passed in the matter of a few weeks.

The German consulted his file again.

"Well, Klein. I am on the horns of a dilemma. And I think you should help me resolve my problem."

Klein said nothing, waited for the scientist to continue.

"One more Jew must be added to the list of those who will be exterminated today."

"Exterminated?"

"Yes, of course."

"But ..."

"Oh, come now, Klein. As a *Sonderkommando* you should be fully aware of what we ultimately do to the prisoners here."

Disciples of Evil

"But I have done all you asked."

"Yes, yes. You have served us well," the doctor agreed. "However, the name added to the list will either be Miriam Klein or Lisabeth Klein. Your wife or your daughter."

The Jew gasped. The women whimpered. Hartmann looked on contemptuously. Brunner sniggered. Dr Von Gruber smiled broadly.

"You, Klein, will decide which one."

"But … But …"

Von Gruber sighed. "Come, come, Klein. You are the head of your family; you must be used to making decisions."

Klein was in a state of shock, trembling and muttering unintelligibly.

Eventually he managed to calm himself and utter a coherent sentence. "You cannot expect me to choose."

Von Gruber frowned. "But I do."

"It is inhuman to have to make such a decision."

"Ah, but you Jews are subhuman."

Klein managed to summon up some defiance. "And you are a monster!"

Naturally, he was punished for it. Hartmann struck him in the stomach with his Mauser rifle. Klein doubled over, then fell to his knees.

He did not attempt to get up. "Please," he begged. "Please!" His hands were clamped together, so he looked as if he were praying, and perhaps he was. "Put my name on the list. I will gladly die in place of either of them."

"How noble." Dr Von Gruber's mouth twisted into a sneer. "However, either your wife or your daughter will go on the list. That is what has been decreed. It is just to be decided which one. *You* will make that decision." Von Gruber observed the man closely; tears ran down Klein's anguished face. "Besides, your name is already on the list of those who will be executed today." The scientist roared with laughter once he had made this revelation. "As I have already said, you have served us well, and you have served your purpose. There is just this one last task for you to perform."

Von Gruber leaned forward. "Well, which is it to be? Whom do you love more? Your wife or your daughter? Which one will you save?"

It was Miriam Klein who spoke. "Alfred, you know what you must do. We had a good life before that evil beast came to power."

That earned her a sharp blow from Brunner's Karabiner 98k rifle. "Watch your tongue, bitch!"

"No!" her husband wailed, powerless to help.

When she had regained her breath, she continued, "We must hope that our daughter will survive this hell and live to have a better life."

Alfred Klein nodded. "Very well. I love you, dear Miriam."

"I love you too, Alfred." She hugged her daughter; all three were crying. "And you too,

Disciples of Evil

my darling child."

Alfred Klein rose from his knees. He was not prevented from moving to his family this time. He embraced them both.

For the first time Lisabeth found her voice. "Mamma, Papa, I love you."

"Ah, how touching." Von Gruber signalled to Hartmann. The corporal opened the door and indicated to the guards who waited outside that they should enter.

"Take them away," Dr Von Gruber ordered.

Dr Von Gruber followed the guards as they escorted the three Jews outside to a walled courtyard where a row of wooden posts waited for them.

"You are not going to make our daughter watch, are you?" Miriam Klein dared to ask the scientist.

"No." Von Gruber favoured her with a smile. "I lied. Your names were *all* already on the list. I was merely conducting an experiment to see whom your husband would choose. I had a bet on the outcome with Brunner." Von Gruber broke off to address the master sergeant. "You owe me a stein of beer, don't you, Brunner?"

"Yes, *Herr Doktor*."

"You see," Von Gruber continued, "you were all already destined to die; just like the rest of your filthy race are."

Alfred Klein howled with rage then and tried

to attack the scientist. He did not reach him. The guards soon battered him to the ground.

Miriam Klein clung to her daughter, but neither had the strength to resist when Lisabeth was pulled away. Miriam collapsed to lie on the gravel, her hand reaching for her husband's, and together the Kleins watched as the guards tied Lisabeth to the middle post.

She stood defiantly, said, "You are the disciples of evil!" and Brunner put a bullet in her forehead.

Von Gruber commended the master sergeant. "An excellent shot, Brunner."

They dragged the weeping Miriam Klein to the post next to her daughter then. Von Gruber nodded. Brunner chambered another round, took aim, and fired.

The woman gave a cry as the bullet struck, and she slumped forward.

"Wait!" Von Gruber halted the guards when they pulled Klein to his feet. "He can go with the rest of the scum instead."

And Alfred Klein joined the other poor souls who had been herded like cattle to meet their death in the gas chamber.

"An interesting result." The scientist concluded writing up his report. He smiled, pleased with the way the experiment had gone.

Brunner yawned.

"You find our work boring, Hans?" Dr Franz

Disciples of Evil

Von Gruber peered at the soldier.

"No, sir."

"Good. There is so much pleasure to be gained from it. Don't you find?"

"Yes, sir." Brunner considered, then asked a question of his own, "You enjoy your work, sir? Having to deal with these scum, I mean."

"I do. I do. Most emphatically. You see, I find myself being in the delightful position of having, what can only be described as, the ideal occupation."

The soldier waited for the scientist to elaborate.

"I get to indulge my most sadistic tendencies all in the name of scientific research. It was a glorious day when our beloved leader came to power."

"A glorious day indeed, sir." Brunner eyed the painting of the Fuhrer that looked down upon them.

Both men smiled and proudly raised their right arms in salute of their leader. *"Heil Hitler!"*

A DOGGIE FOR CHRISTMAS

"Bobbie! Bobbie!" the old lady called.

The brown-and-white Jack Russell terrier ignored her calls and kept running across the recreation ground. His mistress followed, trying frantically to catch him up. Agnes Clements was spry for a seventy-three-year-old, but there was no way she could keep up with her pet. The dog paused to look back at his owner, barked twice, then ran on into the wood.

"Come back here, Bobbie. Oh, you are such a naughty dog."

"Hello, Mrs Clements." Wendy Park waved, trying to attract the old lady's attention.

Until that moment, so occupied with trying to keep up with her pet had she been, that the pensioner had been unaware that her neighbour was also out walking on the rec.

Mrs Clements stopped and waited for Wendy to draw near.

Both women lived on the Woodview housing development. Many of the estate's residents had proved to be unfriendly to the recently arrived Park family, but Mrs Clements always had a smile and a pleasant word to spare.

"Oh." Mrs Clements puffed, out of breath. "Hello, Wendy."

"Having trouble?" Wendy asked.

"I'm afraid I'm getting a bit old for a dog like Bobbie. But at least he gets me out of the house."

A Doggie for Christmas

Mrs Clements smiled, noticing Wendy's ten-year-old daughter. "And hello, young Zoe. How are you today?"

"Fine, thank you, Mrs Clements," Zoe replied. "I've been playing on the swings."

"Oh, how nice. I remember when I used to play on the swings myself. That was a very long time ago of course." The old lady winked at the girl.

Zoe laughed.

A sudden burst of barking from the woods caused Mrs Clements to sigh. "I better go see what he's up to."

"Are you sure you can manage?"

"Oh, I always find it best to come prepared for situations such as this." Mrs Clements produced some dog biscuits from the pocket of her tweed coat. "I'll coax him back." She paused and winked at Zoe again. "Eventually." The old lady gave a wry grin and set off for the wood and her errant dog.

"Bye," Wendy and her daughter chorused. They stood watching her progress and as Mrs Clements reached the edge of the wood, Wendy called after her, "Take care."

Mrs Clements turned to wave goodbye then entered the trees. "Where are you, Bobbie?"

As mother and daughter walked home, Zoe asked, "Mummy?"

"Hmm?"

"Can we get a doggie?"

A Doggie for Christmas

"A doggie?" Wendy frowned.

"Yes, mummy. Please, mummy."

"Well, I don't know. We'll have to see what daddy says."

Later Wendy told her husband, Vincent, about their daughter's sudden desire for a pet dog. "Well, what do you think?"

Vincent looked up from his copy of the local newspaper. "About what?"

"About getting a dog."

Zoe chose that moment to enter the sitting room. "Can we? Can we? Can we?"

"Zoe, were you listening outside the door?"

"No, daddy."

"Hmm. Are you sure?"

"Do you mean, sure that I wasn't listening at the door or that I want a doggie?" Zoe asked, grinning.

"Both, young lady."

"Yes to both, daddy."

"You know why they are called man's best friend, don't you?"

"No."

"Because it's always the man who ends up taking care of them."

Zoe groaned. "Oh, daddy, I'll look after him. Feed him; take him for walks. And everything. I promise."

"Have you tidied your room?"

Zoe looked sheepish. "Um, no."

A Doggie for Christmas

"Well, don't you think you should? How can you expect to look after a dog if you can't even look after your room?"

Zoe pouted.

"Daddy has got a point, darling. Now run along and see to your room."

"If I do, can we get a doggie?"

"Well, it depends on what sort of job you make of cleaning your room. And keeping it tidy."

"One tidy room coming up." Zoe dashed out of the sitting room, up the stairs and began clearing up her bedroom with a dynamism she had never shown before.

"Well, what do you think?" Wendy asked again.

Vincent shrugged. "I don't know. She says she will walk it, feed it and clean up after it, now, but we both know that won't last."

"Yes, but it will be Christmas soon."

"Yes, there is that."

"Well?"

"It'll make a change from having another cat I suppose." Vincent sighed. "Oh, all right then."

Later on Wendy was so impressed with how neat Zoe's room was that she broke the news to her daughter. "Daddy says you can have a dog for Christmas."

"Yay!" Zoe jumped up and down with joy.

"But you have to keep your room tidy."

"I promise I will, mummy."

A Doggie for Christmas

Christmas came early for the Park family.

"Old Mrs Clements has had a fall." Wendy greeted her husband with the news when he arrived home from the restaurant where he worked as a chef.

"Is she all right?"

"She's in hospital."

"Oh dear."

"Do you know what happened?"

"Somehow, she tripped going up some steps. Not only did she hurt her leg and foot, including managing to sprain her ankle, but she also banged her face quite badly and was knocked unconscious. She's all bruised and swollen. She was lucky really; it could have been a lot worse."

"Amazing she didn't break any bones."

"Yes, quite. Thing is, she needs someone to look after her dog – Bobbie. So I said we would."

"Fair enough. I expect Zoe's happy."

"She is." Wendy smiled. "Don't take your coat off."

"Eh?"

"Bobbie needs his late-night walk." Wendy handed her husband the dog lead.

"Oh."

Unfortunately, Mrs Clements picked up a virus while she was in hospital and it was almost a fortnight before she was allowed to go home.

A Doggie for Christmas

"That is good news," Vincent said, when he heard that the old lady had been discharged. "She'll be wanting her dog back then," he added hopefully.

"Well, she'd love to, but she realises she's too old to cope with him."

"Oh."

"She asked if we could keep him."

"Oh."

"Come on, Vincent. Zoe loves having Bobbie here."

"Yes, for two weeks. But do you really think her infatuation will last much longer?"

Wendy laughed. "Oh, I'm sure you'll take care of him if that happens. Man's best friend, remember?"

"I seem to be taking care of him most of the time already," Vincent grumbled.

Vincent was to be proved right. For Zoe, the novelty of responsibility soon wore off.

Wendy stood at the bottom of the stairs and shouted to her daughter. "Zoe!"

"What?" Zoe answered, after Wendy had called three times.

"Have you fed Bobbie?"

"No,"

"Can you do so then?"

"Do I have to?"

"Yes. You do."

"But I'm busy."

A Doggie for Christmas

"Zoe!"

"Can't dad do it?"

"He's busy too. And so am I."

"All right, all right. In a moment."

"Zoe, now!"

Zoe emerged from her bedroom; she was in the process of brushing her long black hair.

Vincent Park came out of the bathroom. "Nice of you to put in an appearance, Zoe. Hope you're looking after that dog." Noticing her hairbrush, he said, "Have you brushed him lately?"

"No."

"Well, don't you think you should?"

Zoe clomped downstairs scowling. "Why do I always have to do everything?"

"But you don't," was Wendy's exasperated retort. "More and more often it's me and your father who have to take care of Bobbie. You seem to have forgotten that it was you who wanted a dog in the first place."

Zoe sighed theatrically. "You never stop reminding me. How could I forget?"

Wendy ignored her daughter's question. "Just hurry up about it. We're supposed to be going shopping. Or is that something else you've forgotten too?"

Zoe waited until her mum's back was turned and stuck out her tongue, then followed her into the kitchen.

Vincent entered soon after. "Make sure you feed him well. We don't want to come home to

A Doggie for Christmas

find he's been eating something he shouldn't again."

"Yes, dad." Zoe scooped dog food out of a tin into Bobbie's bowl

"You might get something nice for Christmas then."

Bobbie had proved to have a prodigious appetite. "He's going to eat us out of house and home," Vincent had declared one day when the family were shopping at the supermarket and he saw just how many tins of dog food and biscuits his wife was putting into the trolley.

They had returned from that shopping trip to find that Bobbie had been chewing on the leg of a chair and torn open several cushions.

"Actually," Wendy said, remembering the mess she'd had to clear up the last time Bobbie had been left alone in the house, "I think in future it would be a good idea to leave him shut in the back garden while we are out."

He was, and much to Wendy's dismay, when the family got home they found that he'd dug up several bedding plants that she had recently planted.

Wendy was woken in the middle of the night by Bobbie's bark. She nudged her husband. "Vincent, wake up!"

"*Gerrorf,*" he muttered, drowsily. Then, "Whassamatter? Whaisit?" after a further nudge.

A Doggie for Christmas

"Bobbie's barking," she whispered, giving her husband a more forceful push.

Vincent groaned. "So I hear."

"I think someone might be trying to break in."

"Humph! The racket the bloody dog is making ought to have scared off any burglars."

"Just go on and check, Vincent." Wendy gave her husband another shove.

"If I must." Groggily, Vincent got out of bed, put on his dressing gown and went downstairs.

He stepped into the hallway and checked the front door. It was secure. Wendy listened anxiously as her husband moved through the house.

A few moments later Wendy heard her husband cursing. "Oh shit!"

"What?" Wendy called.

"Bloody hell! Bloody dog!"

"What is it?"

"The bloody dog has made a mess on the floor. And I've ruddy well trodden in it!"

"Oh. So, there's no burglar then?"

"No!"

"Well, make sure you clean it up before you come back to bed."

Despite all the racket, Zoe slept soundly.

Mr and Mrs Park came to a decision that night.

The festive season duly arrived.

"Glass of sherry, Mrs Clements?"

A Doggie for Christmas

"Yes, please, Wendy. And do please call me Agnes."

"Here you go."

"Thank you. It really is very good of you to invite me around for Christmas dinner."

"It wouldn't be right you spending Christmas all on your own, Agnes. Especially when we've got such a feast lined up."

"I must admit I'm really looking forward to it, your husband has quite a reputation."

A sullen-faced Zoe stomped through the sitting room, slamming the door behind her.

An embarrassed Wendy explained. "We've told Zoe she'll have to wait until after we've eaten before she can open any of her presents."

"I was the same at her age, couldn't wait to open mine. And speaking of presents, I've bought you all a little something." The old lady indicated her bag.

"Oh, Mrs Clements. Agnes, you shouldn't have."

"Nonsense, it was the least I could do, after all you've done for me. How is Bobbie?" Mrs Clements asked before Wendy could protest anymore.

"Oh, he's coming along nicely."

"It's good to hear he's settled in. I suppose he's in the kitchen, hoping for some turkey titbits." Mrs Clements laughed. "I miss him; but he's much too boisterous a dog for an old lady like me."

A Doggie for Christmas

"Not so boisterous now, Agnes."

"Dinner won't be long," Vincent called from the kitchen.

"Another drink, Agnes?"

"I shouldn't really, but if you can't at Christmas, when can you?"

Wendy refilled both their glasses, called her daughter, then led the guest through to the dining room.

"Oh my, you've laid on quite a spread. It looks good enough to eat." Mrs Clements laughed.

"That's the idea, Mrs C." Vincent winked and helped her into her seat.

"Help yourself to vegetables, Mrs C. Now, would you like a leg?"

"Oh, yes please, Vincent."

Vincent began to dish out the Christmas roast. "There you go, Mrs C."

"It smells delicious."

"A leg for you too, Zoe. One for Wendy. And one for me."

"Oh, gosh! You must have a big oven to be able to get two turkeys in. I suppose a big one is a prerequisite for a chef."

Vincent grinned.

"It's not tu—" Zoe began.

"Zoe!" Wendy interrupted, flashing a warning glare at her daughter.

"What?" Zoe pouted.

"Pass the gravy."

SPEAK NO EVIL, SEE NO EVIL, HEAR NO EVIL

Brendan Mulligan didn't recognise the elderly lady who had rung the doorbell. She didn't like to be kept waiting, he judged, by the way she tapped the ground impatiently with her walking cane.

The woman eyed Brendan up and down imperiously. "You must be Brendan."

"I am. And you are?" Likewise, Brendan made a quick appraisal of her. She was large and surprisingly butch; her hair was iron-grey and cut unfashionably short for a woman. Severe was the word that came to mind. He wondered if she were a lesbian.

"Dinah Westcott." She held out her hand. "Marie's aunt."

"Oh." Realisation dawned. "Aunt Di?" Brendan quickly accepted the outstretched hand. The woman's grip was firm and the handshake vigorous.

"That is correct."

"You'd better come in." Brendan stood aside, opening the door wider to admit the unexpected visitor.

"Of course I should."

"Here, let me take your bag."

"No, thank you. It's quite all right. I can manage perfectly."

Brendan was sure she could, despite her

Speak No Evil, See No Evil, Hear No Evil

advanced years.

"This is quite a surprise."

"No doubt. This is the first time I've been back to the old country in many a year."

"What are you doing here?"

Mrs Westcott looked at the young man as if he were an idiot. "News reached me of poor Marie's condition. And you with two kiddies to look after, you can hardly be expected to manage on your own. At times like this, it behoves one to rally round and help out one's family. Even if one has only met one member of that family before."

Dinah Westcott had last seen her niece when Marie had been a child. After Mrs Westcott had left Ireland for foreign climes, Marie had grown up, married Brendan and given birth to two children of her own. Now she was in hospital after being in a car accident.

Brendan showed the visitor into the living room. "Please make yourself at home. What can I get you to drink?"

"Tea. Black, no sugar."

"Make yourself comfortable and I'll brew us a pot."

"Actually, I could use the bathroom first."

"Of course, it's up the stairs, first on the right."

Ablutions done with, and settled in the living room with cup of tea in hand, Mrs Westcott

Speak No Evil, See No Evil, Hear No Evil

enquired about Marie. "Tell me, how is my niece?"

"I'm relieved to say that she's over the worst of it. The doctors expect her to make a full recovery."

"I am relieved to hear it too. What happened exactly?"

"She was driving, and swerved to avoid a girl who ran out into the middle of the road."

"How dreadful!"

"She was lucky really; the crash could have been a lot worse."

"Thank the Lord that it wasn't. I trust the police will be taking action regarding the child's unruly behaviour."

Brendan shrugged.

"Someone, the child or the parents, should be punished for causing such an accident."

Brendan sighed. "I'm just grateful that it wasn't more serious."

"As am I."

"You'll be wanting to see Marie, of course."

"I am most anxious to do so. Hence the reason I have come all this way."

"Then, you must come with me this evening; I have a babysitter booked to look after Harry and Joyce. Visiting hours are seven until nine."

"That sounds ideal. And would you also be able to recommend me a good hotel?"

"No, I wouldn't! You must stay here. I insist upon it."

"Well, if you insist."

"Marie would never forgive me if I packed her Aunt off to some hotel."

"Very well, then that would be most satisfactory."

"Good. Good." Brendan paused a moment, then said, "I must admit Marie has told me little about you."

"Well, no reason she should. I moved to South Africa when she was young; she probably wouldn't remember me too well." Mrs Westcott sipped her tea. "However, what does surprise me is that you didn't know I had moved back to London. I wrote to Marie to tell her."

"When was this?"

"Six months ago."

"Oh." Brendan shrugged. "She mustn't have got your letter."

"It would seem the postal service is still full of shirkers."

"Oh, I don't know, normally we get a very good service."

Mrs Westcott's silent, stony look said what she thought of that.

"You were a teacher, weren't you?"

"Headmistress."

"I do recall Marie described you as being 'strict'."

"That is correct. I believe in discipline. Firm but fair is my motto."

Speak No Evil, See No Evil, Hear No Evil

"They frown on corporal punishment these days."

"And see where it's got us. Your children are well behaved, no doubt. Not like some of the little monsters round where I live. Parents fail to teach their brats how to behave properly." Mrs Westcott shook her head in disgust. "They have no manners, nor respect for their elders and betters."

Brendan was unsure whether she meant the parents, or their offspring. He didn't ask which, but Mrs Westcott seemed to read his mind adding, "Both."

Mrs Westcott replaced her empty teacup upon its saucer.

"Now, where are Harry and Joyce? It's about time I met them."

"Harry's at football practice. Joyce will be round at her friend's house. They'll both be home by six for their tea."

"I see."

"Speaking of tea, how about you have another cup, and I prepare the spare room for you?"

"That sounds like an eminently sensible idea."

Harry and Joyce were presented to their unknown relative when they arrived home. They mumbled shy hellos, and after the evening meal was eaten, they disappeared to their bedrooms as soon as escape was possible. Mrs Westcott went for a lie down too.

Speak No Evil, See No Evil, Hear No Evil

Brendan was getting ready to go to the hospital when the telephone rang.

It was Shona Cameron, the babysitter's mum. "I'm very sorry, Mr Mulligan, but Tracey's feeling right poorly, she's picked up some stomach bug, and won't be able to look after Harry and Joyce this evening."

"Well, that's inconvenient," he said, after the call ended. "I can't leave the children on their own; let me see, there must be someone else I could ask to babysit."

Mrs Westcott held up a hand. "There's no need. As anxious as I am to see Marie, I can wait one more day."

"But—"

"No buts. I can look after Harry and Joyce better than some chit of a girl."

"Are you sure?"

Mrs Westcott sighed in exasperation. "I wouldn't offer if I wasn't. It'll give me a chance to get to know the children better."

"All right then. Thank you. They won't be any trouble," Brendan assured Mrs Westcott.

Brendan had summoned the children downstairs and explained that Tracey wouldn't be babysitting them that evening, and that Mrs Westcott would. This news was met by the usual protests that they were too old to need any babysitter at all.

And after he had left to go to the hospital, the

Speak No Evil, See No Evil, Hear No Evil

children had quickly returned to their bedrooms, saying they had homework to do. Mrs Westcott had settled down in the living room to do some knitting.

It wasn't long before the pop music started blaring out upstairs.

"A little quieter," she called out.

Not surprisingly, there was no change in the volume, as she had not been heard. She went upstairs to find the culprit. The music was coming from Joyce's room. Mrs Westcott made her way along the corridor and banged on her door.

The nine-year-old opened the door sheepishly.

"Turn it down, there's a good girl."

Joyce did so, and Mrs Westcott returned to the living room and her knitting. A few minutes later, the volume resumed its previous level.

Mrs Westcott climbed the stairs again, and this time she went straight into the girl's bedroom and unplugged the CD player.

"Hey!" Joyce cried, from where she sprawled on her bed.

"We'll have no more of that racket. Find something quieter to do, or go to bed."

The girl pouted. Then just as Mrs Westcott was leaving the room, Joyce muttered, "Bitch!"

"What was that?" Mrs Westcott could still move surprisingly quickly when she wanted to and she was back in the bedroom in an instant. She pointed her cane at the girl threateningly.

Speak No Evil, See No Evil, Hear No Evil

"Don't you dare use such foul language again, you little hussy." Then, warning imparted, she turned and stalked from the room.

"Just who do you think you are? You stupid old cow!" Joyce hissed at her back.

This was a mistake. A very silly mistake. Unfortunately, for the children in her charge, Mrs Westcott had grown even stricter than she was when Marie was a child. She had also grown more than a little deranged.

Instead of going back into the girl's room, the retired teacher went to the bathroom and filled the sink with water. She washed her hands using lots of soap, then dipped a glass into the soapy, scummy liquid. Then she went to the guest room, found her sleeping tablets, and added some to the glass. Then she returned to Joyce's bedroom.

Joyce was kneeling on the floor, about to plug her CD player back into the socket. Mrs Westcott left her cane by the door and seized the girl by her long blonde hair. She yanked her head back and Joyce opened her mouth to scream. Mrs Westcott poured the contents of the glass into it.

Coughing and spluttering, the girl was dragged onto her bed and thrust face down upon it. Mrs Westcott sat on her and waited.

When the girl had stopped struggling and Mrs Westcott was sure she was asleep. She went to her knitting bag and retrieved the sewing needle and thread that she also kept in it.

Then she sewed Joyce's lips together.

Speak No Evil, See No Evil, Hear No Evil

After it was done, she stopped to listen at Harry's bedroom door. The boy had been quiet all this time. And that was suspicious in itself.

"Harry?" Mrs Westcott rapped on the thirteen-year-old's door with her cane.

"What?"

She entered his bedroom without waiting to be asked. "Just what are you up to in here?" Mrs Westcott wanted to know. "Oh, you dirty little beast!" she cried, when she spotted the pornographic magazine, and the rapidly shrinking bulge in the front of his jeans. Both of which he was trying desperately to hide.

She grabbed the blushing boy by his wrists and pulled him from the room.

"Get off!" Harry shouted, struggling to break her hold. He was surprised just how strong Mrs Westcott was.

She led him downstairs and into the living room. "Stand with your hands behind your back," she ordered the boy.

Years of authority meant Mrs Westcott was used to being obeyed, and Harry did as he was told. "The devil makes work for idle hands," she snapped, rapidly winding a ball of wool around the boy's wrists, to tie his hands together.

Satisfied he was securely bound, she struck the boy on the back of his legs with her cane. He cried out in pain and fell to his knees.

Mrs Westcott pinched his nose and, when he gasped for breath, she tipped some of her

Speak No Evil, See No Evil, Hear No Evil

sleeping pills down his throat.

Harry was crying. Mrs Westcott hoisted him onto the sofa.

"Stop snivelling, boy." The tip of her cane jabbed towards his eyes, stopping just short of them. "Didn't you know that looking at that sort of disgusting filth will make you go blind?"

Harry was too shocked to say anything.

Mrs Westcott began to rethread her sewing needle, and when Harry's eyelids began to droop under the effect of the sleeping pills, she sewed his eyes shut.

Brendan Mulligan was pleased that Marie's condition was improving. She had been surprised when he'd told her that her Aunt Di had turned up at the house. She'd admitted she had received her letter, but hadn't mentioned it, as, frankly, the woman had always scared her somewhat. Brendan had tried to reassure his wife that her memories were from a time when she was a child and it was natural that she remembered her as being intimidating; she'd see her in a different light now. She'd agreed he was probably right, but even so, she still wasn't looking forward to her visit tomorrow. Seeing how Marie had taken the news of her aunt's arrival, Brendan judged it best not to mention that the babysitter had cancelled and that the children were in Aunt Di's care alone.

He thought that Marie was worrying

Speak No Evil, See No Evil, Hear No Evil

unnecessarily and he called in at the pub for a pint on his way home. He'd had three more before he left.

He arrived home about eleven thirty. Mrs Westcott was waiting up for him. She had a pot of tea ready, and she poured him a cup.

"How is my niece?"

"Improving all the time." He smiled. "And looking forward to seeing you tomorrow," he lied.

"As am I her."

"How are the kids? Did they cause you any problems?"

"They're in bed, of course."

Brendan yawned. "Oh, excuse me." He was suddenly feeling very tired. "Think I'll be in mine soon."

Mrs Westcott waited for Brendan to finish his tea. The tea she had dosed with sleeping tablets. He slumped in his armchair.

"I'm afraid I had to teach them both a lesson."

"What? What was that?" Brendan slurred. He struggled to stay awake, but the dosage was too strong and sleep took him.

Mrs Westcott went on talking, even though Brendan was snoring now. "I blame the parents, no idea how to discipline a child. Marie was always soft, but I would expect better from a man." Mrs Westcott picked up her knitting needles and moved to stand behind Brendan's armchair.

Speak No Evil, See No Evil, Hear No Evil

"Oh, they'll tell you they did nothing wrong. Nothing to deserve their punishment anyway. And it's obvious you'll believe them." Mrs Westcott sighed. "So, I cannot let you hear their lies." She struck then, thrusting a needle deep into each of Brendan's ears and into his brain.

"Well, today has been really rather trying; I'm quite exhausted," she declared afterwards. "I think I'll be able to sleep well tonight." She shook her bottle of sleeping tablets. "Which is good, as I seem to have quite run out of my pills."

FIRST LOVE

Apart from a jukebox playing an old Blues record, Slick's Bar was peaceful. It would soon be busy, alive with people and noise, but for now there was just the one customer.

Errol 'Slick' Hogan was taking advantage of this quiet spell, leaning on the bar, reading a newspaper, and sipping a glass of bourbon.

When the door opened, Hogan raised his bald head, ready to greet a new patron, but the words went unsaid and his expression of welcome turned into a frown as he tried to place a face that was vaguely familiar.

Tall and lean, the newcomer paused to glance around the barroom. It had been several years since he had last been in Slick's, but nothing appeared to have changed much. The walls, where they could be seen behind the slot machines, the vintage jukebox, and the old posters for shows that Slick's had hosted, were still a burgundy colour. The furniture was a mismatched collection of tables and chairs. The pool table still stood over toward the far corner, and at the other side of the room was a small stage, the area in front of it clear. It all looked pretty much how he remembered it. Even Duke Wilson was sitting on his usual stool at the end of the bar with a beer and cigarette.

By the time he had swaggered over to the bar the barman had remembered a youth that used to

First Love

frequent his bar, and recognised him as the man who now stood on the other side of the counter.

"Well, I'll be damned!"

"Been a long time, Slick."

"Well, well, if it isn't Julius Preston."

"That's right. I wondered if you'd remember me." The younger man pulled a packet of Newport menthol cigarettes and a lighter from the pockets of his denim jacket.

"Goddamn!" Duke Wilson grunted.

"Oh, I might be getting on, but my memory's good. I remember everyone," Hogan paused briefly, then added, "and everything."

The last time Preston had been in Slick's Bar he had drunk in a mood of anger and frustration, and he had come to a decision, and after acting upon that decision he had left town. This was the first time he'd been back in nearly ten years.

"So they let you out, huh?" A fair few of those years had been spent in prison.

Preston lit a cigarette, and inhaled deeply. His eyes narrowed. "They did."

"I never thought I'd see you round these parts again, boy."

"Well, here I am."

"Yeah, so what you want?

Preston grinned. "Why, I thought you were never gonna ask, Slick. I'll have a Bud."

After a moment, Hogan nodded, and said, "Very well."

First Love

While Hogan was getting his beer from the cooler, Preston turned his attention to the other man present. "How you doin', Duke?"

"Mr Wilson to you," the old-timer grumbled.

Preston laughed. "Good to see you ain't changed none, Mr Wilson."

"Here you are." Hogan opened the bottle and placed it on the bar. "So why you come back here then?"

Preston handed over a five-dollar bill, took a drink, shrugged and said, "Why not?"

Hogan laid out his change. "You'll be visiting your mother?"

"Sure. She still at the same place?"

Duke Wilson gave a gasp, his cigarette balancing precariously on his lower lip.

Hogan gestured to the old man to remain silent. "No, she's moved on."

"Oh? You know where I can find her?"

"Yeah," Hogan paused, "she's got a nice quiet place in the cemetery."

"What?" Preston brought his bottle of beer down on the counter with a bang. "She's dead?"

Hogan nodded. "Been seven years now."

"Well, damn!" Preston didn't seem particularly upset. "Well, how about that? They never told me."

He took another mouthful of beer. "Well, what about any of the old crowd I grew up with? Any of them still around?" He drew on his cigarette.

First Love

"Mmm, yeah, how about that girl who used to work here? Gloria. Yeah, Gloria."

Wilson gasped once more. "You ..." he began to say, but Hogan interrupted.

"You'd like to see her, would you? I remember you had the hots for her."

"Yeah, why not? Just for old times' sake." Preston grinned. "Or are you going to tell me she's fat and married with half-a-dozen kids?"

"Nope." Hogan took a swig of Bourbon. "You should look her up."

"Alright then, I will. Where would I find her?"

"You could say she's off Broadway."

"Huh? What you saying man?"

"You know Nevin Alley?"

"Oh, yeah. Yeah, I know it."

Hogan leaned closer. "A place off of there, some call it the Pleasure Palace."

"Oh!" Preston's grin grew broader. "Oh right." He laughed. "Yeah, Gloria Lucas, the Pleasure Palace, that sounds about right."

Preston finished his drink. "Well, it was good to see you gentlemen again, but I think it was time I made a move. Gotta look up a pretty face from the past."

Moving towards the door, Preston's thoughts were already elsewhere, and he didn't pick up the cold tone in which Hogan said, "I'm sure she'd like to see you."

Preston turned before leaving, took a final drag on his cigarette and dropped it to the floor. He

First Love

trod on it, and with a laugh said, "I always knew she liked to show a guy a good time."

"But not you, hey, boy?" Hogan muttered as the door closed.

"Goddamn, Slick," Wilson gasped in astonishment. "He doesn't know, does he?"

Julius Preston made his way along Broadway, this was the heart of the red-light district, and he passed adult bookshops, peep shows, porno cinemas, sex shops, strip clubs, and massage parlours. The street was bright with flashing neon lights, loud with thumping music. He ignored the strip-club barkers, the pimps and hustlers, even the prettiest streetwalkers couldn't tempt him.

Before today it had been a long time since he'd thought about Gloria Lucas. When he was a teenager he spent a lot of time thinking about her; had thought he was in love with her. It had been an obsession, and in a way she was partly responsible for him turning to a life of crime. Curiosity aroused, Preston was eager to see her again.

Nevin Alley lay between Albert's Liquor and the Hardcore Video Store. Preston rounded the corner and wrinkled his nose as the smell hit him.

"Damn!"

He had to abandon his customary swagger to avoid the foul-smelling puddles of piss and

First Love

vomit, and the broken glass that littered the alleyway.

Nevin ended in a rubbish-strewn courtyard, in which stood a single three-storey building.

The building was a dirty grey, smeared with green stains; its windows were broken or boarded up. There were no gaudy neon signs or flashing lights, in fact, from the front, the place looked to be in darkness, and abandoned. A painted sign above the entrance proclaimed it to be the Palace Hotel.

"What the hell is this?"

Obviously the hotels around here were of the sleazy variety – their principle trade being hookers and their johns, rooms by the hour, no questions asked – no one respectable would want to stay in this area, but this certainly wasn't what he had been expecting.

As Preston crossed the courtyard, he wondered if Slick Hogan had been playing some kind of joke on him. If he had, he would make the bald-headed bastard pay.

He tried the front entrance but found it locked, so he went to the rear of the property.

The back door swung open at a push. Preston took out his lighter and Newports, lit one of the menthol cigarettes, and stepped cautiously inside.

Rats scattered. "Shit!" One ran over his foot and he kicked it away.

First Love

Preston looked around him. He was in a kitchen, but the only thing that had been cooked there recently was crystal meth.

He sighed, this wasn't looking good. "Now you've come this far, Julius, you might as well check the rest of this dump out," he told himself.

The only exit from the kitchen led into a corridor with two doors on either side, and a staircase at the other end.

Preston paused and listened carefully. He could definitely hear signs of life. He tried the door to the left.

"Piss off!" A voice from the gloom snapped. Preston could make out several bodies lying on the floor. The room stank of stale sweat and farts, that, and the snoring, convinced him to look elsewhere.

"Damn place is more like a flophouse than a whorehouse!" Preston muttered.

He pushed open a door on the right. The room was lit by smoky candles, and the air was thick with dope. People sat around smoking spliffs, others were injecting heroin.

"Welcome to the Pleasure Palace, man." The speaker – a skinny white kid wearing a baseball cap back-to-front – giggled. "We got drugs. We got girls upstairs."

"I'm looking for Gloria. You know where I can find her?"

First Love

The white kid frowned, looked puzzled. No one else showed any interest in Preston's question.

"Is she here?"

"Yeah, yeah." He giggled again. "Yeah, like I said, she's upstairs."

Preston nodded, and moved towards the staircase. Behind him he heard what sounded like someone vomiting, then more laughter.

One of the remaining doors opened and a wrinkly old white woman emerged in front of him. "Looking for a girl, dearie?"

Preston's expression was one of distaste. "Yeah, Gloria, not you!"

"Oh, Gloria is it? Popular girl is Gloria."

"Yeah, she always was." Preston recalled sourly.

"Well, it's fifty bucks if you want to go upstairs." The woman smiled. It wasn't much of a smile, as she didn't have many teeth left, and they were rotten.

"Fifty?" Preston laughed dismissively. "Yeah, right. Outta my way, Granma!"

"Oh no, sonny!" Arms folded, she blocked his way. "Just because you're a strong young man and I'm a frail old lady, don't go getting the idea that you can just go up there without paying,.."

"Oh? And why's that?" That was exactly what Preston had been thinking.

"Because I've got this!" The old woman suddenly produced a Smith & Wesson Model 29

First Love

revolver. "They don't call me Dirty Harriet for nothing!"

"Okay, okay. Easy now. I'll pay. Fifty you say?"

Harriet nodded. "That's right."

With the gun pointed at him, Preston knew he had no choice, so he slowly took out his wallet and handed over the cash. He would make sure he got it back later.

"Alright, dearie. Gloria was it?"

"Yeah."

"Well, she's in room number one, but she's with someone at the moment. You can either wait – why not partake of one of the substances we can offer? – or you can go on up and watch. Or maybe even join in," she added with a wink.

Preston was getting impatient now. "I'll go up."

"Oh, you are keen! Well, you could try one of our other girls if you're that desperate. Candy in room number three could show you a thing or two if you have a taste for the unusual ..."

Preston snorted, and pushed past the old woman. As he climbed the stairs he could hear her cackling behind him.

There was no spy hole in the first door, but from the grunting and groaning coming from behind it, it was clear what was going on inside. The old woman had said it was okay to watch, so Preston pushed the door to reveal a bare room lit by a single electric light bulb, the only furniture

First Love

was a dirty mattress. The mattress was occupied, but from where Preston stood in the doorway all he could see was a white guy's bare, fat hairy ass going up and down.

The door had made a noise as it swung open but the man hadn't heard it over his grunts of exertion.

"Eww, man!" Disgusted yet curious, Preston took a step forward. A floorboard creaked and the white guy finally glanced over his shoulder.

They both spoke at the same time. "What the fuck?!"

Even though several years had passed Preston realised he recognised the white guy. Even after all this time he'd know that ugly face anywhere. It was that bastard: Larry Danning.

Now it was his cigarette that balanced precariously as Preston stood watching in open-mouthed astonishment. He'd come looking for Gloria Lucas, he hadn't expected to find Larry Danning still on the scene as well.

That was just his first surprise.

Danning kept thrusting despite Preston's intrusion. Finally he shuddered, giving a last grunt, and rolled off of the woman beneath him.

The second surprise left Preston dumbstruck.

The woman Danning had been fucking was not surprisingly completely naked, but she was lying on her front, head turned to the side, her long black hair obscuring her face.

First Love

But what had shocked Preston was the fact that the woman had neither arms nor legs.

She was just a head and torso. She was gasping and moaning. Though Preston was unsure whether it was in pleasure or pain.

"What the fuck, man?" Preston finally muttered. "Is she …"

"Who are you?" Danning lay on his back, glaring up at Preston. "What the fuck do you want?"

Preston threw down his cigarette and ground it underfoot. "What the fuck are you doing, you fucking pervert?"

Danning laughed. "Pervert? That's rich coming from you, standing there watching like some grubby Peeping Tom. Is that how you get your kicks?"

Even though Preston started to advance angrily towards him, Danning seemed unafraid. His lip curled into a sneer. It made his face even uglier. "What's the matter with you? Don't you want to fuck her? Can you only get it up by watching?"

At last the woman spoke. "Who is it, Pappi? What's going on?" Her voice was harsh, damaged somehow, yet familiar.

"Don't worry, baby; it's just some jerk-off!"

Her laugh was more of a gurgle than a giggle. "Ooo, Pappi, does he want to jerk off all over my pretty face?"

First Love

"Well, let's see." Danning sat up, rolled the limbless woman over onto her back, and pulled the hair away from her sweaty face.

"Oh my God!" Preston came to a sudden halt as he saw her scarred body, the mutilated chest where once had been a pair of breasts he had fantasised about as a teenager. She had been beautiful, but she would never be considered that again. Her face was badly marked with old wounds, but despite the damage Preston knew her.

Julius Preston had found Gloria Lucas.

Despite his revulsion he peered more closely at her ruined face and realised that she was blind. That that was why she hadn't recognised him.

She had been Preston's girlfriend when they were teenagers. He had been in love with her.

Until she had dumped him and started going out with Larry Danning.

She had betrayed him, and she had betrayed her race.

The bitch!

At first, Preston naively hadn't known what Gloria had seen in Danning. But later he realised it was because he was older, more experienced; had a job, a flash car, and more money. That was what she had found so attractive about him, as it certainly wasn't his looks – the ugly white bastard!

"What happened to her?" Preston whispered.

First Love

Danning reached for a can of beer and gulped some down before answering. "Car crash."

"What?" Preston looked at him sharply.

"It happened a long time ago now. I was driving. I'd had a few, but I wasn't drunk despite what they said. There was something wrong with the car, I couldn't control it." He paused to take another mouthful. "I couldn't stop. I thought we were going to die. I was a mess, had several broken bones, but it was nothing to what my poor Gloria had suffered. It was a miracle she lived." He shook his head. "Maybe it would have been better if she hadn't, but I still love her."

Gloria's mouth twisted into the resemblance of a smile as she heard his words. Saliva dribbled from between her lips.

"Don't I, baby?" He turned to kiss her scarred cheek.

As Danning spoke the past came rushing back to Preston. At the time, he had thought Gloria was the love of his life. But then she had started dating Danning. That had been bad enough, but then he found out Danning was involved in the swinging scene and had been sharing her with his friends. She'd got a reputation for being a freak in the sheets, and the thought of all those white guys having her when she'd never even sucked him off, never mind let him get into her panties had been too much.

He remembered that night he'd sat drinking alone in Slick's Bar consumed with rage after

First Love

he'd found out. Gloria had hurt him, hurt his pride, and he wanted to hurt her in return, not physically, but by making her suffer. He'd wanted to kill Danning. Or at the very least harm him badly. And that night he came to a decision about how he would do it.

Preston was working as a trainee mechanic at Hobson's Garage, so he knew just what to do. After leaving Slick's he had gone over to Danning's place and tampered with his car. That flash motor was Danning's pride and joy. If his sabotage didn't lead to Danning's death, it should at least wreck his car. Figuring the cops would have him at the top of their list of suspects, Preston had skipped town rather than hang around to see the outcome of his actions. He just wanted to get away and get over Gloria, and he did it by hooking up with a couple of hot blondes – after all, if a little interracial sauce was good for the goose, then it was good for the gander too – and a whole load of booze and drugs.

His first love and his first criminal act – it had all seemed so important to Preston once, but there had been many, many women in his life since Gloria and many more crimes, and it had all faded in importance as time had passed.

Danning was speaking again. Preston had missed some of what he'd said as he'd been lost in his memories of the past.

First Love

"By the time I got out I'd lost my job. I owed loads of people lots of money, and had started drinking heavily. And the Pontiac was ruined, that car was my prize possession." He laughed bitterly. "Things went downhill from there, but at least I still have my Gloria."

Danning drained the can he was drinking and tossed it aside. He belched, licked his lips and reached to Gloria's crotch, rubbing her clitoris.

Preston watched, and despite Gloria's grotesque appearance he found himself becoming aroused. Danning spread her wet pussy open. "Well, what are you waiting for? Disabled people are entitled to a sex life too, you know!"

Preston licked his lips and unbuttoned his jeans.

"She likes to know men still find her desirable," Danning said to him.

Then, "You're going to enjoy this, baby," to Gloria, as Preston got his rapidly stiffening cock out.

Preston knelt on the mattress. His was bigger than Danning's, and it was time to let the prick-teasing bitch know what she'd been missing out on all those years ago.

MORE HORRORS FROM MORTBURY PRESS

FOR THOSE WHO DREAM MONSTERS

Eighteen tales by Anna Taborska.
With illustrations by Reggie Oliver.

Face your fears and embark on a journey to the dark side of the human condition. Defy the demons that prey on you and the cruel twists of fate that destroy what you hold most dear.

Winner of The Dracula Society's Children of the Night award.

*

THE BLACK BOOK OF HORROR

An eleven volume anthology series of the horrid, the horrific, and the horrible.

www.ingramcontent.com/pod-product-compliance
Ingram Content Group UK Ltd.
Pitfield, Milton Keynes, MK11 3LW, UK
UKHW041943230426
12048UKWH00008B/96